Broken Wings, Soaring Hearts

BEVERLY A. ROGERS

CRIMSON
ROMANCE
F+W Media, Inc.

This edition published by
Crimson Romance
an imprint of F+W Media, Inc.
10151 Carver Road, Suite 200
Blue Ash, Ohio 45242
www.crimsonromance.com

Copyright © 2013 by Beverly A. Rogers

ISBN 10: 1-4405-6978-9
ISBN 13: 978-1-4405-6978-4
eISBN 10: 1-4405-6979-7
eISBN 13: 978-1-4405-6979-1

Cover art © 123rf.com

Dedication

This book is dedicated with much love to God, and to my family, Bret, Jon, Lindsey & Hailey. You are the loves of my life and you always make me want to be better. My cup runneth over.

"Follow God's example in everything you do
just as a much-loved child imitates his father."
Ephesians 5:1

Acknowledgments

Eva Shaw, you are the mentor everyone dreams of. Your teaching, advice, and friendship have changed my life. Thank you.

Jennifer Lawler, thank you for believing in *Broken Wings, Soaring Hearts* and bringing me into the Crimson Romance family.

Julie Sturgeon, your editing is right on. I don't know how you do it but you are amazing. Thank you.

CHAPTER ONE

"Hailey Holman, you are the most unreasonable child God put on this earth."

Hailey wiggled her slender frame from beneath the twin engine Brown Skycat IV. A film of gray dust mixed with drying Texas mud coated her dark shoulder-length hair and ran down the entire backside of her denim work shirt and jeans.

"Oh? You *think*?" Like she'd never heard *that* before. She made a playful lunge at her mother's starched yellow apron. "As you remind me daily, I *am* my daddy's daughter."

"*Stop that!*" Rinnie Holman squealed and dodged her daughter's greasy grasp. "Call it off. I mean it. That man has no business coming here."

"If you're referring to Jack Stinson, 'that man' is coming in for an interview, and he might just have all sorts of business here." She narrowed her eyes in mock sternness. "And I expect you to be on your best behavior."

Hailey turned and plucked a towel from the wooden workbench to scrub at her hands, examining yet another broken fingernail. Seven down, three to go. Her nails looked like they've seen the ugly side of a cheese grater. If her mom and sisters got a look at the shape her toes were in, there'd be an emergency pedicure intervention. A crisis of infomercial proportions. Thank goodness her work boots kept that scary secret.

"Do you think I'm playing, Hailey?" Her mom's sharp words broke Hailey's random thoughts. "He is not welcome here."

"Mom…" The vibrating cell phone in her pocket saved them both from another "I have to do this and it really is for the best" speech. She slung the towel over her shoulder and dug for the phone. "Hello."

"Ms. Holman? Jack Stinson."

The voice she'd been anxious to hear. *Don't back out, don't back out.* She projected her thoughts at him: Do. Not. Back. Out.

"Hey, Jack. Where are you?"

Her mom let loose with an exasperated sigh loud enough to scare buzzards off their roadside dinner in the next county.

"Just turned onto two-twenty."

Hailey swiped her glistening forehead with the end of the towel on her shoulder. "Great. You're about forty-five minutes out. You'll lose cell service for the next forty minutes of that, so better make any last minute calls while you can."

"Thanks for the warning. Looking forward to meeting you and seeing the operation."

"I feel the same. Drive safe!"

Hailey flipped her phone closed and eyed it with disbelief. *I feel the same?* She shook her head at herself and tucked the phone back into her pocket, pulling the towel from her shoulder and tossing it aside to rest on the workbench.

A faint warmth crept to her cheeks. How un-Hailey like. The butterflies swarming around in her stomach must have eaten up some brain cells. She turned her attention to intentionally pretending to ignore her mom's outraged glare.

The glare. Her mom was famous for it. Within the family circle, of course. Nobody in the community ever saw it. Hailey knew it was intended to poke a hole in the resolve in her heart. By now her mom should know nothing was going to displace the determination—or the excitement—whirling around inside of her.

"Mom, it'll be fine. You'll see."

"Call him back right now. He's not coming here."

"Can't. He's already in the dead zone. No service."

"What do you know about this person? He could be a thief for all you know. Or a killer. Is that what you want? You could be putting me and your sisters in grave danger."

"He's not a thief. Or a killer, Mom." Her voice was kind but firm. "We're not in any danger. You know good and well I've checked him out."

"How? On that intranet thing? People lie about everything on there all the time."

"Yes, they do, Mom. You are so right."

Rinnie's argument was momentarily defused.

Hailey continued. "And I've helped Dad run this place since I could crawl up into the cockpit with him, so again, Mom, you can't give me one good reason why I can't run the business on my own. With the help of Mr. Stinson. Hopefully."

"Run it on your own? What makes *you* think that?" her mom scoffed. Distressed eyes seemed determined to pierce Hailey's heart. "You've been gone since August."

Hailey's mouth fell open in automatic self-defense, but no words followed.

It was true. When she left in August to attend the University of Houston, she had no idea that two months later, her life—all of their lives—would be changed forever. It wasn't her idea to continue her education in the first place. It was Dad who had convinced her she had to do it.

Maybe it was because after working together full-time for awhile, he sensed a restlessness in her that she herself was unaware of. Or maybe it was because her mother had never given up on the idea Hailey would go to college and pursue a "meaningful" career—as in something that would tie her to a desk, with four walls painted a seriously practical shade of taupe. To Hailey that would be a jail sentence. Torture. She knew she'd end up climbing those perfectly painted walls.

But Web Holman had insisted, so she went. If his oldest daughter planned to make the business her life, she needed an education to go along with all that on-the-job training she'd gained after high school. She'd chosen business administration. It seemed the best fit to benefit the family business they both loved so much. So that was the plan. But by mid-October, he was gone.

Hailey gave her mom a tender smile and fought to keep stinging tears in check. No one ever talked about it, but her dad had confided in her once when her mom was on a tangent: 'Honey, your mom has a good reason to be scared of our flying. She won't share anything about it but she was in a plane accident many years ago.'

Hailey had questioned him many times, wanting to know more. All he would say was "please don't mention it: just respect your mom's feelings and try to understand where she's coming from."

In Hailey's eyes, God had already shown her mom how He would protect them. To live a life filled with fear? That was wrong. We have to have *faith*. "Flying and planes are in my blood. I'm just like him, remember, Mom?"

Her mother stood in quiet reflection, tugging without mercy at Hailey's heart. "You got his pig-headedness."

The sudden tenderness in her mom's voice caused her to look squarely into the older woman's eyes.

"Mom…"

"You're going through with this." It was a statement edged in distressed resolution. "After all my begging and pleading and reasoning. You're going through with it. Oh, Hailey. You cannot run this airport without your father. And I am so weary of trying to beat that point into your stubborn head. Can you not hear what I'm saying?"

Hailey sucked in a deep breath and released it through puffed cheeks. Leaning against the Skycat, it seemed like she was the only one who wasn't trying to run away. How could everybody else just want to give up on what dad had worked so hard to build? Isn't that what was really important, now? He'd put everything he had into this business. How could her mom—and the rest of her family for that matter—not *see*?

"Hailey! I'm waiting for an answer."

She returned her attention to the woman before her. Her mom standing with defiant hands on narrow hips. A scene becoming more and more familiar these days.

"Yes ma'am?" Hailey stomped a puff of dust from her work boots. "Did you just say lunch is ready?" She tried to bedazzle and shift her mom's mood with an extra toothy smile.

"No, lunch is not ready," came her mother's exasperated reply. "I'm not feeding you another meal until you come to your senses. And stop smiling like that."

"Like what?" She kept smiling, with an urgency to rekindle the playfulness that held the anguish at bay. It was Hailey's way of dealing with the sadness. That, and a five-pound bag of chocolate kisses never hurt either.

She gave her hands one last wipe against worn jeans, looped an arm through her mom's, and took a step across the concrete floor, giving the older woman's arm a playful tug. "Come on, Ms. Rinnie. I'm too weak from hunger to carry you."

The set of Rinnie Holman's jaw made Hailey unwind her arm and wrap it gently around the thin, rigid shoulders instead. Leaning her head against graying curls, she lifted her own eyes to scan the enormous Texas sky filtering through the double metal hangar doors.

A much needed early morning rain had settled the normally dry and dusty earth surrounding them, but Hailey knew that even in mid-April, the scorching southern sun would soon bake the soil and the air will be humid and broiling again.

Six months. It seemed like six minutes and at the same time six-hundred years. She could still hear his deep voice boom across the yard at her, urging her to look up—look up and see that God had blessed them with yet another beautiful day. Storm or sunshine, it was always another beautiful day to Dad.

She usually had to agree. And if she didn't right off, he had a way of making her realize it before the day was through and God "pulled the starry curtain of night down on their little piece of the earth" as he was fond of saying.

A smile touched her lips. Her dad was an adventure-maker. A risk taker. A godly man. Not a soul who knew him questioned Web Holman's integrity for a moment.

If only her mom's eyes would open. If only her mom could see the promise of another beautiful and inspiring day canopied by an endless sea of dreamy blue sky. Why couldn't she grasp the magnitude of the opportunity they had here?

Sometimes it was hard for Hailey to remember that the same hangar and everything in it that held an enormous source of strength for her, held a great deal of pain for her mom. Even that vast, azure sky seemed to trigger her mom's sorrow.

Hailey had spent countless hours with her dad, soaring into the wild blue yonder. It was there that she learned how much her dad loved their Creator, and there that he passed that love on to her, filling her heart and mind with stories of God's grace.

Her attention returned to her mother, following the older woman's gaze across the yard to the house the Holman's called home even before the birth of their oldest daughter, twenty-six years ago.

Just last night Hailey had broken the news to her mom: she'd placed an ad in a trade journal, hoping to find a replacement for Mr. Edwards, the airframe and power plant mechanic who'd worked for her dad.

That went over like a sack of tators on a waterfall.

"Why do you insist on doing this?" Her mom interrupted Hailey's thoughts again, digging a tissue from her apron pocket and dabbing quickly at tears forming in her hazel eyes. "Your father wouldn't want you to do this either," she warned, tucking the tissue back into her pocket.

"We both know better than that, Mom. The plan was that I would come back to help Dad with the business, remember? And that's what I'm doing. Only…without him."

She breathed away the tightness in her chest as she remembered the day two months before his death. He had stood at the head of the dinner table, chest puffed proudly, with that familiar twinkle in his eye, making the grand announcement: "When Hailey returns home an educated lady, she'll take my place as president and CEO of The Blue Yonder Flyers."

Hailey had immediately protested. That was, and always would be, his position. She just wanted to be there to help him. To share the business with him. To do the job they both loved.

She certainly wasn't sticking around because she loved Barnes, Texas. Hardly.

Barnes, Texas, population seven hundred, thirty-three. Seven hundred, thirty-five if Paul and Neal Watson counted as human beings. Hailey's cheeks warmed. Dad never let her get away with talking bad about anyone, even if it was about those sorry, good for nothing…

Rinnie interrupted Hailey's thoughts again as she wheeled to face her, grabbing her daughter by both shoulders. "Your father is gone and things have changed around here. It's useless to hang on to what might have been. *It's over, Hailey.*" She ripped the words out emphatically.

"Mom, I'm sorry, but this business is Dad's dream. Mine and his."

The weariness in her mom's eyes stabbed at Hailey's heart, but she knew what she had to do. "Don't you understand that it's my dream and God's plan for my life?"

Her mom's hands dropped heavily from Hailey's shoulders. "It may have been some dream to the two of you, but for the past twenty-nine years, it was my nightmare. I prayed every day he'd stop flying. And as for your life plan, have you bothered to ask the Lord or are you so full-steam ready to have it your way that you'll do this regardless!"

Hailey felt an instant rise in blood pressure. "Mom!" The sound of her own voice rose to meet her level of frustration, and she pulled in a full breath to calm herself, adding as softly as she could, "I know God's plan for my life, and I'm sorry if His plan and your plan don't match."

Her mother's eyes blazed. "Is this the way you honor your father's memory? By dishonoring your mother?" The anguish in her mom's voice was almost enough to start the emotional avalanche unsteadily perched on top of Hailey's heart.

Focus on the goal, she reminded herself, and everything will work itself out. *It's up to me to keep the dream alive. It's the only way to keep Dad with us. Mom will come around. She has to.*

"Mom, I love you so much. And I'm sorry you can't seem to understand what I know in my heart I have to do. If I could go back to October and change things, I would. Things might have been different if I had…if I…" she fought to steady her voice as she searched her mother's face. "Can't you just be happy that we have a part of Dad here?"

Her mom's stony silence answered loudly.

But Hailey couldn't give up. "You know flying had nothing to do with his death." She halted, searching her mom's face for a shred of understanding that obviously hadn't come in years. Ever hopeful, Hailey prayed for something, anything, that would finally break that one impenetrable wall between mother and daughter. She wrestled with the lump in her throat.

"Mom, he had a heart attack. He could have had it sitting in the front row in church."

"That's enough!" Rinnie Holman covered her ears with her hands, as if not hearing the words could erase the heartbreaking loss they shared. "I won't hear another word about this airport, and that's final."

Without giving Hailey another chance to speak, Rinnie dropped her hands from her ears and twisted away from her daughter, stomping toward the well-worn trail leading to the white one-story farmhouse.

Hailey allowed her heart to follow her mom's deliberate steps along the yellow path of bricks between the metal building and the house. Caked and dirty now, she knew that as soon as the scorching Texas sun came back around to dry the mud from the early morning shower, her mom would carefully sweep clean each step, leaving a fresh bright path linking the two parts of her life.

She shoved her hands deep into her blue jean pockets and watched Rinnie, the angry steps pounding in rhythm to the beat of Hailey's broken heart. A deep sigh escaped Hailey's lips as the heavy metal storm door slammed.

Hailey let out another deep sigh. Her mom would come to realize this was meant to be.

Her heart burned with renewed determination. "And there's no messing with what's meant to be," she promised with a determined tug of the heavy storm door leading into the kitchen of the home where she was raised.

CHAPTER TWO

He leaned forward and rested strong forearms across the padded steering wheel of his Jeep, stretching his neck from side to side. Jack Stinson felt like an escape artist.

"Escaped." The word tasted ominous. But good.

He ground the word out again through clenched teeth. "Es… caped."

His grip tightened on the steering wheel.

If it wasn't for the Stinson stubborn streak he'd come by so honestly, he never would have lasted five years with his dad in the first place. Watching the business turn into something he didn't recognize was torture.

"Something had to give. And it was no longer going to be me."

He let his eyes survey the unfamiliar road before him. "I'm talking to myself," he stated bluntly, slipping dark shades from his eyes to rest on top of his head.

"Who does that?" Squinting through weary eyes at the green pastureland around him, he kept on talking. "Anybody who's been around Marshall Stinson too long, that's who."

Jack fought the dull ache in his heart. Deep down, he was more sad about leaving than he wanted to admit, even to himself. But if he'd stayed…if he'd stayed he'd have become another paper war casualty. Buried beneath mountains of forms and templates, waiting for the inevitable landslide. Buried and trapped. Never to be heard from again.

"Okay, now that's real dramatic." He covered his strained eyes once again with the shades. "I'm done with all that drama."

The anxious drone of wheels against highway failed to drown the sound of his dad's enraged voice. "You walk out that door, Jack, and you will no longer be worthy of the Stinson name. You forfeit all rights to Brown Aeronautics and to this family."

It stung deep. But the rejection from his dad's words was nothing compared to the pain in his mom's eyes when she heard her husband's harsh words for their oldest son.

Marshall Stinson was good at throwing out some pretty heavy verbal jabs. And Jack had shielded his mom and younger brother for a long, long time.

His hands held a death grip on the wheel. What his dad had managed to do to a four-generation family business should be illegal. It had become everything Jack hated. Now. Hurry. Fast. Faster. Cut corners. Cut quality. Shave a little integrity here and there.

"No!" One hand rose and beat down hard on the leather dash.

His nerves throbbed. The burden placed on him by his position as vice president of Brown Aeronautics—and by his father—had pushed him beyond human limits. It was hard to know what his limits were anymore. When his mom started insisting he get out, he knew it was past time to go. He *never* thought he'd hear that come out of her mouth.

Jack reached into the pocket of his sports shirt to retrieve the map he'd jotted down during an earlier phone conversation with Ms. Holman.

Hailey Holman. He let a light smile ease across his lips. What kind of boss would she be? *If* he got the job.

When they'd talked she seemed calm and straightforward. He could hear a smile in her voice. She just might be the Anti-Marshall Stinson.

Perfect!

He started to unfold the paper but returned it to his pocket instead. No need to check the map. Barnes exit, continue west off

Highway 220, to FM Road 1207, right turn past the service station on the right, and down about six miles. Second house on the right.

After all, he was used to maneuvering himself around the big city of Dallas, nine miles from his hometown of Cryder. He certainly wouldn't have any trouble getting around in a town the size of Barnes. As always, he'd done his research; less than eight hundred people lived there. The Stinsons had almost that many people working for them at Brown Aeronautics.

Hard to believe places like Barnes still existed.

He drew his lips in thoughtfully. A place like Barnes, Texas, could be exactly what he needed to get his life back. Goodbye, rat race.

Rolling down the window, Jack leaned his head into the wind. Air. Fresh air. Jack shook his head. In true Marshall Stinson style, his dad had kept him at the office well after midnight with a typical mountain of last minute "this can't wait" paperwork. One last show of power. One last-ditch effort to control his son.

Dependable Jack. The responsible one. He'd never leave anybody hanging and his dad knew it. He knew he'd take care of everything before leaving this morning.

The air helped. Some. He pulled himself back upright and readjusted his shades. He already missed his mom and brother, Eric.

Man. Jack sucked in another deep breath and let it out slowly. And kept on driving.

In spite of the exhaustion he felt from the long hours and long drive, a restless energy overtook Jack. He'd given Brown Aeronautics all he had and now he felt worn out, burned out and stressed out; and he just plain wanted out.

"Let's get this new life started." *Today.*

He reached for the knotted muscles between broad shoulder blades and worked up and down his neck. That same stubborn tension spot had irritated him for months. Or was it years?

He drummed his thumbs on the steering wheel. *If he'd wanted me to stay so bad, you'd think he'd open his eyes a little.*

He drummed harder. *He wanted me to be too exhausted to leave today.*

The drumming stopped and he straightened his back.

Not a chance. Sheer determination and a hard head had kept Jack focused.

Jack left as planned. On time.

He made the last turn onto FM 1207.

"I'm going to stop thinking about it. Right now."

He drove without a thought for half a second.

Keep peace in the family at all costs. Who's going to do that now? What about the people I care about? They'll have to contend with Dad on their own.

He was tempted to turn around. He could. If he wanted to. Which he certainly did not.

"People move on. Families move forward. I did what I had to do." Then why did he feel like a rat?

He forced his eyes and his thoughts to return to the landscape around him. With every mile putting Cryder, Texas, behind him, he should expect to be more at peace. The tension should be somewhere back there in the dust. A distant memory in his rearview mirror.

Durn. Mom and Eric should have come with me.

If he could remember back far enough, surely he'd find childhood memories of snow cones and water gun fights on the back lawn.

His eyebrows arched in thought as he maneuvered down the road, trying hard to conjure up a memory. Any fun-being-a-kid memory.

"Nah. Not there."

Jack traveled the last few miles in silence, his lips pulled into a straight, solemn line. He allowed his mind to slip into a semi-contented place.

Next stop: contentment. Tranquility. Like the beauty of the scenery in front of him.

"God be with you." His mom had clung to him and blessed him with those words as he was about to leave.

God be with me.

Something between guilt and sadness worked at his heart. God had been forced into the backseat of his life years ago.

Backseat? Jack had to be honest with himself. More like the trunk.

"Well," he reminded himself. "This is all about changing my life. Who knows…" A light shrug lifted and dropped his shoulders.

And he saw it.

The white, one-story farm house on the right side of the road. Neatly trimmed trees and long, gravel drive. Had he seen this place before? He thought hard. No. Maybe just in his mind, while picturing an ideal life.

Jack's nerves started unwinding and he felt suddenly very comfortable. Instantly welcomed and at home. Two wooden swings facing each other caught his eye, hanging from gleaming silver chains on the front porch. The sight promised simple pleasures he'd missed for so long, like sitting around doing nothing except thinking and staring at the world around him.

He raked a hand through his hair.

Wooden swings beckoning to me? I must be even more starved for tranquility than I realized. He felt his neck tighten again. *Downright ridiculous.* That was his dad's favorite saying for anything that wasn't his own idea or didn't revolve around Brown Aeronautics. But sometimes it fit Jack's own state of mind, too.

Jack turned into the driveway, trying not to let one inch of these new surroundings escape his notice. Old Jack stayed back in Cryder, head down, full-steam ahead. New Jack was determined to enjoy the beauty of the emerald grass alongside the driveway. Something he'd come to take for granted back home.

Ah, this was his idea of a tranquil place to enjoy life. The winding yellow brick path along the front of the house lined with periwinkles and roses. And begonias, his mom's favorite. The railed porch stretched the full length of the front of the house, holding those two wooden swings and a well-used oak rocker.

He continued to roll his Jeep up the drive, where a full-grown chocolate Labrador Retriever stood guard on the top step, eyeing the approaching vehicle with more than a passing interest.

This is living, he marveled. He let out a low whistle and tried to contain his eagerness.

As he was about to tap his brake, the scene shattered dramatically as a young woman bolted through the front door with an ear-piercing shriek he heard even with his windows up. The storm door closed steadily behind her.

The Lab hopped around her legs, taking his eyes from Jack's whereabouts for a mere second.

Jack stopped, turned the ignition to off and reached for his briefcase on the seat next to him. Opening the Jeep door, he stepped onto the gravel drive, not taking his eyes from the raucous on the porch.

The crunch of rock beneath his feet made him grow more anxious.

The woman glanced his way at the sound of his car door closing. She waved, keeping one hand free to continue her romp with the dog. "Come on up," she yelled, motioning for him to open the milk-white iron gate at the end of the walkway.

Jack's attention turned from the enormous dog and settled on the young woman with the shoulder length dark hair. She stood comfortably in well-worn jeans and denim work shirt.

He moved closer, taking a moment to readjust his eyes from the beauty of his surroundings to the beauty of the vibrant, smiling woman standing before him.

What a picture, he marveled to himself. A gorgeous—and unexpected—picture.

* * *

With surprised interest and her pulse beating a little quicker, Hailey regarded the man approaching the walkway of her childhood home.

She gulped hard.

This guy didn't look anything like his voice sounded. Not that she was in the habit of speculating about voices and faces. But Jack Stinson...*hello*!

She issued herself a stern reminder. Not interested. Remember?

The full extent of her interest was that this guy who responded to her ad in *Flyer's World* was a good mechanic. And a good person.

She'd never settle for less than a good, hard-working employee. And he had to be a Christian. Handsome was *not* on her list of employee qualifications.

He's really, really attractive.

Heat crept from her collar bone to her forehead.

She shoved the absurdity of the thought aside. So, he was nice looking. Big deal.

She took a few steps toward him, with the Lab matching her closely, step for step.

"Jack Stinson." She extended her hand and offered a welcome smile. She wanted to release his hand quickly.

She didn't.

Her cheeks colored again. *Am I staring?*

"Miss Holman?" Jack returned her stare openly after shifting a brown leather briefcase to his left hand and clutching her outstretched one. "Miss Holman?" he repeated.

"That's me. Miss Holman. Hailey. Hailey Holman. Call me Hailey." She released her grip on his hand and stooped to give the brown dog an affectionate tussle on the head. That sounded lame, she admonished herself.

"And this here is Kisses. Hershey Kisses." She kept her eyes on Jack.

At his name, Kisses jumped playfully at the stranger. Jack stepped back, briefly surprised by the exuberant friendliness. He reached out to offer a brief pat to the big, sturdy head.

"Kisses, down!" ordered Hailey. She cast a glint of surprise her dog's way. "You big hound. You know better than that. What's wrong with you? Sit!" She tucked a wisp of dark hair behind her ear. "You must really have a way with animals, Jack. Kisses doesn't take to just anybody. He really likes you."

Kisses seated himself obediently at Hailey's feet, peering up at her through doting eyes.

"I'm sure glad he likes me. He's a big, *big* dog." Jack reached out to stroke the dog's head again, apprehension giving way to obvious admiration.

"Yeah, he's a monster." Her eyes twinkled with amusement. "I think you're safe though; he's still pretty full from eating the meter reader this morning."

"He's a very beautiful dog. You really shouldn't make him out to be such a brute."

"You're right," she teased. "He's very sensitive. I shouldn't hurt his feelings. Especially while the two of you are bonding."

She regarded Jack with genuine interest. *Stick to business. Don't get personal. Don't get into his personal life. Mechanic. Good person.* "You didn't grow up around animals, did you, Mr. Stinson?"

Well, sticking to business lasted about a micro-second.

"No, not at our house." He scratched Kisses behind an ear to the dog's obvious delight. "My father thought pets were useless. If there wasn't a way for them to make you money, there was no reason to have them around." He shifted his hand to the dog's other ear. "Maybe if he could have figured a way to put them on the assembly line we could have had a house full of them."

"That's sad." She offered him a sympathetic smile. "I couldn't imagine growing up without pets."

He shifted his attention fully to her. "My mom rescued a cat once. Just a kitten. Under the hood of her car, if you can believe that. White with the most distinctive gray paws. Ended up giving it to my grandparents, but it was fun for the whole two hours we had it."

"Did you ever get to play with it again?"

He nodded at her, a little like she was a co-conspirator in his big deception. "Snuck over when my dad was out of town a couple of times. They had that cat for years."

"We've had dogs, cats, birds, fish, hamsters, turtles, horses, and Chester. The goat."

"That must have been interesting."

"It was." Her mischievous laughter rippled the air. "My father let Chester in the house one time and you should have heard my mom. On second thought, maybe it's a good thing you didn't. Poor Chester ended up under the kitchen table, terrified. And when animals get excited or scared…ugh. They make a mess."

Jack offered her a wide grin. "I could only imagine what would have happened at my house." He raised his eyebrows inquiringly. "Where'd you come up with Hershey Kisses for this guy's name?"

"You might as well know." She met his grin head-on. "I have a significant addiction to chocolate." She tousled the dog's ears again. "Doesn't he remind you of a humongous chocolate bar with teeth?"

Kisses appeared to be smiling, and with his tongue hanging out of his mouth, the clear view of sharp white teeth contrasted with rich brown coloring.

"Hershey Kisses," he repeated. "I like that. All kidding aside, I'm sure he's a great watchdog. Look at the size of those teeth."

"Personally, I rarely put kidding aside."

His expression questioned her.

"I was making a joke, Jack. You know, ha. L-O-L. A joke."

He shifted his briefcase to his other hand. "Okay. That was a good one."

She clasped her hands in front of her and rocked back on her heels. Her humor seemed to be underwhelming him. Or Jack Stinson was playing hide-and-seek with his sense of humor. Maybe he was just as anxious as she was to get on with the interview. Maybe she should force herself to tear her stare away from that strong, square jaw and the dreamy eyes she knew had to be hiding behind his shades.

She refocused herself, boldly meeting his gaze without a shred of interest.

Somewhat.

Maybe his seriousness wouldn't be so bad, she reasoned. Her mom might like his maturity. Maybe his serious side would help her get past the dark wavy hair and dimple in his left cheek. Maybe she'd just see him as strictly an employee.

What color are his eyes? She strained to see through the dark tinted glass of his sunglasses.

Oh, who cares, she reprimanded herself. The important thing was that he could do the work. As long as he was willing and able, he was her man. Or the business's man.

Jack's deep voice redirected her thoughts. "When I drove up it looked like you were in some sort of distress."

"Oh, that's right. I *was* in distress. Actually," she pushed her hair back, "I was squirting lime in a glass of iced tea, and a stream of juice flew into my sister's face. Accidentally, of course." She chuckled. "I'd *never* do anything like that on purpose. So, my sister maliciously grabbed a lime to retaliate, and that's when I ran outside. I think you're the one who saved me when you drove up." She kicked the urge to add "My hero" to the curb.

"I'm glad I was on time then." He offered her another solemn nod.

She gave him a curious look. "Okay, I just have to ask you. Are you being cautiously serious or guardedly business-minded? Is this you, or maybe a slightly interview-infused-with nervousness you?"

He pulled his sunglasses from his face and she saw the intriguing brown eyes that had been hidden from her view. "Both. Maybe. What's the difference?" His expression said he really wanted to know. "I'm pretty accustomed to focused business relationships. Successful businesses are built on solid, mutual goals and respect."

She blinked at him.

"I'm doing the over-serious thing again, aren't I?"

She simply nodded.

"Ok, actually, where I just came from—the business I just left, the owner my dad—insisted that to make a business relationship work, there had to be a strict level of professionalism. Total separation of personal and professional lives."

She thought she saw a flicker of disappointment in those beautiful brown eyes. "And you believe that, do you?"

"Whether I believe it or not is irrelevant." He offered her a confident grin. "It's what I've been taught, Miss Holman. This job is important to me, so if I get the chance, I'll give it my full attention. Now, that doesn't mean I can't loosen up a little bit. I sure don't want a formal workplace."

He continued, "Other than, of course, to make sure the work is done and done right. I just left a business where it had become all work and absolutely no fun and I sure don't agree with that philosophy entirely. But it's not advantageous to either one of us to mix too much business with pleasure. Not if we're going to do this right. But I do want to, like I said, enjoy what we're doing."

They stared at each other for a moment.

She held onto a chuckle. "Okay, I gotta tell you, Jack. That's not gonna work for me."

He seemed taken back before letting loose with a deep sigh. "Alright, you got me. I'm a bottom-line kind of guy. But like I said, this position is very important to me."

"Glad to hear that. About the job being important, that is." She arched her eyebrows mischievously. "So your business style is no-nonsense, serious and stuffy. No offense."

"None taken," he assured her. "But I think you're misunderstanding. I do think we have to be serious. But, having said that, I don't want to come across as stuffy. I think I'm more serious-focused. Or at least that's how I see myself."

"So if I accidently laugh while I'm being serious-focused, you're ok with that."

"Sure. That would be ok." She almost laughed again when he caught himself. "Oh, you're good."

Hailey gave him two thumbs up. "You're catching on." She eased into a smile. "We could have fun in spite of yourself, Jack Stinson."

"Hire me and we'll see if we can come to a mutual agreement regarding workplace decorum."

Well, she mused, at least he was trying his hand at her brand of humor.

"Jack, my father believed work should be fun and so do I. We've always been successful and good at what we do, and enjoyed every minute of it. You and I could both have some interesting adjustments to make."

He nodded his agreement. "It could certainly be a disastrous combination."

"Or," she countered him with a spark of a daring in her voice, "It could be a match made in Heaven." Her brain went into scramble mode. "A business match, of course. That's what we're talking about. Business."

Nice recovery, she mentally jabbed herself.

His eyes regarded her for a long moment before his lips broke into a decidedly more comfortable grin. "You do have a way of putting things, Miss Holman. And you're right. I could use a good dose of loosening up."

"And 'some' people say I could use a good dose of seriousness." She leaned toward him, lowering her voice. "But I've never been good at taking my medicine. If you're around here long enough, you'll find that out." She dug in her jeans pocket and retrieved two silver wrapped chocolate kisses, offering him one.

He declined with a shake of his head. "No, thanks."

She unwrapped both chocolates and held them to her lips. "Good, more for me." She popped them both into her mouth with obvious pleasure. Comfort food. "Okay, enough small talk."

Still chewing, she motioned for him to follow her. By the time they reached the porch steps, she had devoured the candy. "Let's get on with the interview, Jack. That'll ease some of your pain."

"My pain?" He gave her an odd look.

"Another joke. Ha. Ha?" She gave her head a good-natured shake. "We're gonna have to do something about this serious case of seriousitis." She stepped onto the first step. "I think you're just out of practice. Be thankful it's not terminal."

He followed a few steps behind. "So you think there's hope for a hopelessly serious bull-headed workaholic."

"There's *always* hope." She opened the storm door for him. "Welcome to our home." She made a sweeping gesture through the open door.

Jack stepped across the porch and stopped before the door. "There's some beautiful workmanship in this house," he said, running his hand along the framework of the door.

She nodded in agreement, letting her eyes roam lovingly over the solid wooden porch.

"My dad built this."

He nodded his approval. "Amazing work. Quality. Rare to find these days."

"That's for sure." She stepped inside the door, still holding it for him. "You won't find much around here that doesn't have my dad's own special touch."

He moved forward but then turned to take one more look around the porch. "Did your father really build this entire house?"

Hailey nodded proudly. "With help from my uncle and a few old cronies around town. You've heard of an old-fashioned barn raising? Well, this home was an old-fashioned house raising. A real community effort. My father had many, many friends."

"Had?"

"He passed away in October."

"Oh, I'm so sorry." His concern was genuine. He stepped onto the blue flowered rug inside the door. "I was under the impression that he…that this was…a family business."

"It is. I'm still here," she stated, letting the storm door close lightly on its own behind them.

"Well, I know, but I mean, are you planning to…"

"Run the business myself? You bet I am. Hopefully, with your help." She motioned for him to follow her into the living room.

"I see." He took slow steady steps behind her steady, energetic ones.

"You seem surprised." She stopped in front of the sofa and turned to face him. A faint smile tipped the corners of her lips. "Have you been talking to my mother?"

"Pardon?"

"Nothing. I suppose it seems strange that I could take on such a huge project, me being a *woman* and all."

"No, of course not. I don't think I have any doubts that you're very…capable."

The amused smile faded from her lips and was replaced by a solid, determined grin. "I'm more than capable, Mr. Stinson. My father put a great deal of trust in me with the business while he was alive. I didn't let him down then, and I don't intend to let him down now."

"I'm certain you're more than able. It's just that in this world today, a beautiful woman…" His face turned the deepest shade of tomato and he redirected his comment. "You're obviously intelligent. But to run your own base station? That's tough work. I can't picture it." He crawfished around the words. "Right now. Yet, I guess."

"You can probably picture me in the kitchen a lot easier, right?"

"I'm getting into so much trouble here. I didn't mean to insult you but that's about all I've done since we started talking. I'll be honest, in our business my father never hired women in a leadership capacity." He held up both hands in self-defense. "I'm not saying that's right or wrong, I'm just saying that's the way it was. We had admin assistants, and a few worked in the warehouse, but as far as decision making processes were concerned…"

His somewhat embarrassed voice faded as he seemed to search for the appropriate words. "Not that I agreed, like I said, but my father believed men were captains of the business world. My mom was strictly in charge of household affairs. Entertaining, decorating, things of that nature."

"And your sisters? Were they banished to the galley as well?" Her eyebrows raised in his direction.

"No sisters. Just me and a younger brother." More heat rose from his neck to settle in his cheeks. "I know it sounds archaic, but, yes, if I'd had sisters, I'm certain they would have been raised the same way."

She hoped her face remained friendly yet certain. "That's a really sad story, Jack. My dad involved me in the business from the very beginning. He taught me that women were just as *capable*," she emphasized the word, "as any man. He'd have waited a long time for a son to work with since he ended up with three daughters."

Her steady words ran at him in a wave of determination. "He encouraged me to take my rightful place in the business, and I can't tell you how thankful I am he did."

Jack looked as if someone had stuck a sword into the pit of his stomach. "Sometimes that's something to be thankful for and sometimes it's not."

She eyed him with curiosity, and motioned for him to take a seat on the pale pink and white chintz sofa.

This guy had to work out.

Not because his chocolaty brown eyes intrigued her.

Or because of the uncharacteristic way Kisses had taken a liking to him.

Or because she sensed he was a good man, but somewhere inside of him, he was dealing with something really painful. Just like she was.

But mostly, she soundly notified her practical side, because if he didn't, her mom would bird-dog her every move to keep her from finding another potential employee.

CHAPTER THREE

Jack continued to study the woman standing before him. Something about her was different from anyone he'd ever met. Different in a good way. A really good way.

That would be great, he reminded himself, if he was looking for a woman in his life right now. Which he wasn't.

He had to get his feet on the ground and stay focused on the immediate objectives at hand. Find a job he enjoyed. *I can't wait to get my hands dirty again.* Like in the early days when he followed his great-granddaddy around the hangar, handing him tools and learning how to fix planes.

That's how Jack liked it. That's what he seriously missed. Before shareholders and marketing specialists. Before bigger, faster, impersonal service. Before it became something Jack didn't recognize or want to be a part of anymore.

He admired Hailey Holman instantly. Her obvious commitment to what she believed in was commendable. Her sense of humor was attractive, but man, he didn't need any complications right now. And those blue eyes could definitely spell complications.

She brought him back to reality with a resolved nod. "Let's talk about getting you to work. I'd like to get started as quickly as possible, before the ERA is revoked and I have to go back to the kitchen where I belong."

He took the seat she offered and set his briefcase on his lap. "Great idea," he agreed.

As soon as the words left his lips, he felt the crimson in his cheeks intensify. "I didn't mean it was a great idea to go back to the kitchen. Or that your rights could be revoked. What I meant was…"

She silenced him with an uplifted hand. "Ease up, Jack. I know what you meant." She shook her head as her lips once more broke into an amused grin. "Honest, Jack. If you're going to work around here, you have to lighten up. You take everything so literally." The grin intensified.

"If you think men are superior to women in the workforce, it'll be my most enjoyable task to show you otherwise." Her sky blue eyes held a glint of challenge. "We all have our own strengths and weaknesses—men *and* women. That's how God made us."

Jack wanted to climb down into that hole he'd so effortlessly dug for himself. From now on, he'd keep his big mouth shut. If she was going to be his boss, that was actually fine with him. He believed it didn't matter whether a person was male or female, just so they could do the job. But he could hear his father now. This would be one more thing for Marshall to ridicule his oldest son about.

He quickly flipped the clasp on his briefcase with an efficient snap, welcoming the thought of talking business. Certainly that was a safe topic. Maybe he wouldn't embarrass himself further if they just stuck to what he knew best: airplanes and profit sheets. He hadn't had anyone to banter back and forth with like this since… *ever*. That spark in her eyes when she laughed stirred something inside him. It was something like a cross between guarded intrigue and a magnet pulling him toward her. Even her teasing half smile drew him in and made him want to smile back at her. But the most fascinating thing was…she didn't seem one bit aware of how amazingly gorgeous she was. This woman was going to keep him on his toes. Or frustrate him to no end. He wasn't sure which.

• • •

Hailey found herself secretly enjoying Jack Stinson's uneasiness. Not in a mean way of course, but she enjoyed the good-natured teasing and joking that once filled their home. Her sisters could be fun, but it wasn't like when their dad was with them.

The semi-straight-faced, bordering on formal, applicant in her living room seemed a perfect candidate for some rounds of lighthearted fun. *Potential is what he has.*

Hailey tossed him a jovial smile before heading for the brown leather recliner across from the sofa. Her dad's favorite chair had been a comfortable refuge, especially during the past six months. The soft leather still smelled like him.

On her way, a glimpse of her reflection in the large beveled mirror hanging above the chair caught her off guard.

Who is that?

Her disheveled reflection made her suddenly wish she'd taken the time to brush her hair and change from her dirty work clothes before he arrived. She must reek of oil and dirt from the morning's work under the plane. Her eyes canvassed the sparkling hardwood floors. They picked up the pristine reflections of the crystal vases filled with fresh begonias resting on Grandma Holman's antique side table.

She must look like a sack of tumbleweed in comparison.

Stop it! No big deal, she thought, feeling a bristle of indignation.

But this was, after all, an interview. A business meeting. It would merely have been more *professional* to present herself in a more positive light. Professionally speaking.

Not that she felt the need to make a good impression on Jack Stinson, or anything. It was nothing like that.

What was it her father always said? "Do the best with what you've been given, and leave the rest to the Almighty."

She shook off the uninvited thoughts traveling through her mind.

Besides, she thought with a touch of annoyance, I don't have to defend myself to myself.

She slid her fingers through tangled hair, wishing a comb or brush would drop from the ceiling fan above her. She caught him staring at her expectantly. "I've been sanding a few spots on the belly of the Skycat this morning. Getting ready to paint."

She felt flustered. What was wrong with her? She never acted like this. Giddy. Like a diva. That's what she called her sisters: divas. She raked her bangs back impatiently. *Since when do I have anything to prove? Don't be a woman right now, Hailey. Be a businessperson. Looks don't matter, anyway, remember?* "I'm sure I look like a wreck," her mouth announced without warning.

His only comment was a slight squint in her direction.

She smiled an uncharacteristically self-conscious smile at Jack, eyeing his pocketed pullover shirt. He looked perfectly presentable, with an unusually sharp crease in his designer jeans. *I'll bet he irons everything.* She had friends from college who ironed everything and Hailey had always teased them. Jeans, bed sheets, pajamas… of course, if that's what they wanted to do, more power to 'em.

She gave herself a mental jab in the ribs. Her cheeks continued to burn. Oh, for heaven's sake. She hadn't blushed in years, and now…consistently in less than one hour. She stretched her hand out in his direction. "How 'bout that résumé?"

He retrieved a crisp professional folder from his briefcase and handed it to her. Taking it from his hand, the sight of her younger sister, Felicia, and her mother poking their nosey heads around the corner from the kitchen caught her eye. Hailey gave them a brief, tight-lipped grimace on the sly, hoping Jack didn't pick up on the two eavesdroppers behind his back. Felicia held a hand pressed firmly against her own mouth to stifle a giggle, while Rinnie Holman shot her oldest daughter daggers through impatient eyes.

Hailey paused. "Uh, tell you what." She reached across to lay his résumé on the coffee table between them. "I'll get us some iced tea. We can sit on the porch. It's safer…*better*! It's better. Airy. Nice fresh air." She hopped to her feet. "Sugar? Lemon or lime?"

"No sugar. Just a squirt of lemon." He gave her a wry look. "In the glass, please, not in your sister's face."

She nodded as she hurried to the kitchen, his first attempt at levity escaping her notice. At any moment her mom could huff into the room and tell the poor guy to get lost. Or worse. Rinnie Holman was typically a kind Christian woman, but when it came to planes and the business—that tongue!

And it would be like Felicia to come right out and tell him about his adorable brown eyes and nice shoulders. Neither of them could be trusted to show tact. If anyone was going to do anything embarrassing in this family, it would be Hailey—and she wanted to keep it that way.

Hurrying to the kitchen, Hailey closed the door behind her. She stood, hands on hips, her face twisted into a warning grimace.

"What is wrong with you two?" she half whispered, her tone agitated enough to get her point across. "He could have turned around and seen you both acting like a couple of loony tunes."

"Oh, I'm sorry I'm such a wreck," her sister fawned. "If I'd only known you were such a hottie I would have dressed up in my best coveralls, or at least brushed my ratty hair…" Her sister fell over her mom in a fit of giggles.

Rinnie pushed her youngest daughter away. "Well, I don't think it's funny. Stop wasting that young man's time. His services aren't needed here, and if you don't tell him, I'll tell him right now."

Hailey shushed her mother as she hurried to pour Jack's tea, giving it a quick squirt of lemon. Without thinking, she aimed the lemon at Felicia and issued an ultimatum. "You either keep Mom quiet, or you get this again."

Felicia let out a louder cackle at Hailey's threat. "Well, I'll just go in and tell that man that you want to give him a big fat kiss on the lips." She directed a loud smacking sound at Hailey. "So are you gonna ask him to marry you? Can I go in and ask him to marry you?"

Hailey gathered Jack's glass along with the watered-down glass she'd poured for herself earlier. "First of all, stop acting like a sixteen year old. And second, you just do that, Miss Diva, and I'll tell him that those cheerleading sweaters that you so amply fill out aren't totally, shall we say, you."

Felicia gasped. "You wouldn't!" Her mouth gaped open. "And they're only lightly padded." She gripped her mother's arm. "Aren't they, Mom? And I am sixteen, so I can act sixteen if I want."

Hailey turned to leave the kitchen, issuing one last order with a stern frown. "You two behave and stay here in the kitchen where you belong." She closed the door between the kitchen and living room with her foot and made her way into the living room with a tall glass balanced in each hand.

She handed Jack his tea. "Here. Let's go," she said hurriedly.

"Is everything all right?" He cast a curious look over his shoulder, toward the kitchen.

"All right? Oh, sure, fine. Everything's great." She took a long, deliberate sip of tea, retrieved the résumé from the coffee table where she'd left it, and headed for the front door. Maybe her mother wouldn't follow them outside and try to scare him off. Maybe if they worked fast …

Jack followed her, briefcase and glass of tea in hand, back out onto the porch.

"This is better," she insisted. "Much roomier, don't you think? Lots of fresh air out here."

He glanced at the vast outdoors around them.

"Pick a swing, any swing." She motioned to the two swings facing each other, and without waiting for his choice, plopped herself on the swing facing the front door. Just in case.

He seated himself opposite her on the empty swing and set his briefcase beside him on the seat.

She held the paper before her and let her eyes scan the lines quickly. Born on…graduated from…worked for…ah. There it was. The million-dollar question. With the million-dollar answer sitting right beside it.

Single.

She raised her eyes and found him watching her with intent patience. She gave her swing a slight push with her work boot. Any self respecting boss would need to know that. For insurance purposes. Yeah, uh-huh, insurance.

"Your resume looks really good. Let me tell you more about our operation."

He settled back intently as she continued.

"We have two crafts, both of which you're familiar with, since your company designs and manufactures the Skycats." She smiled at him. "I love that plane, by the way. My dad thought it was the best."

She went on. "As we discussed on the phone, I need a certified A & P who can do routine maintenance and repairs. It helps that you're a pilot, too, even though according to your résumé, you're not up on your hours. We'll have to recertify you so you can help me with the flying. My father and I stayed unbelievably busy. When I left for school, he had to turn down quite a bit of work. I want to make that up to him."

She set the résumé in her lap, suddenly aware but pleasantly surprised, at how well she'd regained her business sense. Somewhere during the conversation her brain had recovered and she felt decidedly more in control. As she was supposed to be.

"It'll take both of us working hard. We'll be the nearest *reputable* base station in a sixty mile radius." She decided to hold off telling him about the irreputable station for now. Neal and Paul Watson. Why spoil a perfectly good interview before she absolutely had to? It was enough that she'd have to tell him that her mom wasn't thrilled about reopening.

Not thrilled. Understatement.

Obviously, neither situation was something she'd be able to keep from him, for obvious reasons. Nor would she want to. But she couldn't help but dread the thought of it.

She gave herself another giant push and tucked her legs underneath her. "We rent hourly to individuals, or we pilot the crafts ourselves for business and pleasure trips." She let her eyes follow a hummingbird to a feeder at the other end of the porch, and then fixed her gaze back on his face.

"You and I would be the only staff pilots, so as my father and I did, we would try to book clients so that one of us could be here at all times for refueling and to take calls." She stopped to let her words sink in. "Sound good so far?"

Jack gave a firm nod of his head. "We discussed salary and hours on the phone, so I'm clear on everything, I believe. This job sounds like exactly what I'm looking for. I'm sure you'll want to check my references."

She gave him an incredulous look. "You think you're sitting on my family's porch without being checked out first?" But until he stepped out of his vehicle and she got a look at him, it hadn't occurred to her to check his marital status.

He gave a slow, knowing nod. "Of course. I should have guessed you'd already have done that."

"So, you're ready to start today? After lunch?"

"Yes, ma'am. Just point me to the nearest hotel where I can plant my stuff and get a bite to eat, and I'll be back as soon as possible."

"You could drive into town and eat at my Uncle Frank's diner, they have the best sweet tea and chicken fried steak you've ever had. But I'm sure you're exhausted from the drive and lunch is already cooked and ready here." She wrinkled her nose at him. "And the only hotel within forty miles is the Barnes Roach Motel." She waited for a chuckle but he only nodded.

"It's not really called that, by the way. In case you were wondering, I was making one of my famous jokes." She hesitated again and let it go. "I'd hate to send you there."

She hadn't intended to offer, but something told her it was the right thing to do. "We have a nice cottage near the hangar. You're welcome to bunk there until you find a place." Her mouth twisted into a wry smile. "It's either that or the aforementioned Barnes Motel." She gave an exaggerated shudder. "Want to see the cottage?"

"Gratefully. If your family doesn't mind." She folded his résumé and tucked it into her shirt pocket as she rose from her seat. "No, of course not! Why would they mind? You're more than welcome to stay here." Not a total fib. *She* was glad he was there. And as far as the rest of the family goes, they'd definitely be on board once they got on board with all the rest of the stuff they weren't crazy about right now.

"I'll stay in my sister Lindsey's room. She's off at college right now. Except for some weekends." She made her way down the porch steps with Jack matching her step for step on their way to the back side of the house. She stopped midway on the gravel drive. "There it is. Isn't it great?"

He let out a low whistle and gave a nod of agreement. "This is the little cottage you mentioned? It's a miniature country estate!"

She tipped her face to the blue sky, basking in the compliment as well as the rays of the warm Texas sun. "My father and I built it."

His mouth gaped open and he looked from her to the cottage and back to her. "Are you serious?"

She nodded, her thoughts filtering back to the first day when she walked arm-in-arm with her dad as they followed the brick path around the house, surveying their handiwork. It was to be her own home, and the two of them had designed the plans together.

The wrap-around porch was her idea. The double doors into the kitchen were his. She hated to let anyone else move into her home, but it made more sense than expecting Jack to find a place in Barnes right away. The roach-infested Barnes Motel was out of the question. Besides, she wanted the person she hired to be close to the aircraft. This was the best she could do for now. It was worth the sacrifice. She knew her father would agree.

Jack broke her thoughts as he marveled again at the intricate woodwork across the front of the house. Before she could respond with another thank you, the ear-piercing roar of an old mufflerless pickup zoomed past the house, shattering the peaceful countryside. In an instant, a longneck beer bottle flew from the passenger's side window, soaring the long distance from road to Jack's Jeep, where it smacked fiercely against the rear headlight. The hit was followed by the outrageous wild yelps of the truck's occupants.

The unexpected ruckus hung in the humid April air like an ominous cloud. Hailey turned her stormy eyes to face the utter shock on Jack's face. Even from where they were standing, there was no question about the damage to his Jeep.

"I guess I should tell you about the Watson brothers." She choked the words out between clinched lips. "Our competition."

CHAPTER FOUR

Both of Hailey's fists were clenched tightly at her sides. "Kisses can't stand those boys." She attempted to keep an even tone. "He can hear them coming from ten miles down the road. You should see how crazy he gets when they have the audacity to actually drive into our driveway! I can't even tell you how upset that poor dog…"

Jack held up a hand to silence her, feeling his ebb of calm slowly fade. "The competition? Those…those…" He couldn't seem to find a word. "They threw a bottle!" He proclaimed it as though she hadn't witnessed the assault with her own eyes.

She offered him an apologetic grimace. "They did."

They stepped back toward the Jeep and eyed the shattered tail light. Jack felt a rush of blood through swelling veins course through his neck and up to the top of his head. Of all the crazy outbursts he'd ever witnessed, this one had to be the most thoughtless, reckless—his mind scrambled for the perfect word—idiotic. As Kisses slowly regained his composure inside the house, Jack wondered how long he'd be able to maintain his.

The non-threatening existence he thought he'd found? Shattered. Just like the broken glass at their feet.

He worked to keep his cool on the outside, but his insides boiled. His eyebrows arched in Hailey's direction. Her words finally registered. "What do you mean, they're the competition?"

She didn't look any calmer than he felt as she dug her hands into the pockets of her jeans.

She gave an angry shake of her head. "Those boys make me furious! Remember I told you we're the only *reputable* base station within a sixty-mile radius? Well," her lightning blue eyes followed weaving tire tracks down the dusty country road. "There went the unreputables."

He studied her face. "Those guys?"

Her disgruntled nod answered the question.

Without waiting for further explanation, he did a closer damage inspection, the annoying crunch of gravel beneath his shoes echoing the irritation he was sure both of them felt.

Hailey followed closely behind, the frown on her own face deepening with each step they took around the vehicle.

Jack bent to run a hand along the backside of his Jeep. He straightened his back, hands firmly placed on his hips. "They have good aim, I can say that for 'em."

"Not hardly." Her dark eyebrows slanted in a frown. "They were aiming for your head."

"They were what?" Before she could answer, he held up his hands to stop her. "Never mind. I don't want to know." He dropped his hands in disgust.

"Well, don't take it personally. It's me they're mad at. I know that's small comfort…"

He interrupted. "*No* comfort."

"Okay," she conceded. "*No* comfort. But the deal is, Neal and Paul don't want me to reopen this base station." She kept her eyes on the broken bottle lying at their feet and added under her breath, "That seems to be a running theme around here."

"I may regret asking," I'm sure I'll regret asking, he thought warily, "but what in the world is going on around here?"

He looked at her as if he actually expected an answer.

"Well, Jack, it's a really long story, and one you really don't need to concern yourself with. I really can take care of all of this." She added under her breath, "Hopefully."

"Listen, if I'm going to be associated with this business, I need to know what's going on."

She sucked in a deep breath and blew it out. "Alright, I guess we should have this talk. But I'll give you the abbreviated version." She gazed across the meadow to the other side of the road, prolonging the inevitable.

"When we were in the fourth grade, Neal and Paul's daddy died."

He halted her with a raised hand. "First, if you're starting all the way back to the fourth grade, this sounds like it's gonna turn into the unabbreviated version. And second, all three of ya'll were in the fourth grade together? So they're twins?"

She shook her head. "No. Just…well, that's a long story, too."

He gave the back of his head a rough scratching and urged her to continue. "All I have right now is time, so. Go for it."

"Mr. Watson to that point had kept as tight a rein on those boys as possible, but after he was gone, they nearly ran poor Ms. Carleen to her own grave."

"Hard to imagine." She met his sarcasm with a knowing nod.

"Right. Anyway…" her voice died away as she took a deep breath and continued. "The family had been struggling financially for some time." Her eyes grew misty and she struggled to keep her voice calm. "My dad gave Mr. Watson odd jobs here and there to help out when he could." She shrugged sadly at the memory. "But he was proud, you know? There was only so much he'd allow my dad to do. One morning my dad gave him some work trying to pull a flatbed out of the mud in our back pasture. Later that evening he had a heart attack."

Hailey worked to recover her previous composure as her mouth twisted into a frustrated frown. She transferred her gaze between Jack and the battered Jeep. "Anyway, Neal and Paul were nothing but bullies to me and my sisters, even before they thought we caused their dad's death. But after…" She gave a long, exhausted sigh. "It's been *torture*."

"I know what you're thinking," she said at his silence. *You wanna run.* "But it really did get better until just recently. Both boys left for a while and worked as crop dusters for a small outfit on the other side of Houston."

"A Watson brothers break for Barnes."

She nodded adamantly. "You'd better believe it. That was the most peaceful this county has been since they were born, I think." She stooped to begin carefully picking up glass. "Of course, that job fell through. You can't stay smashed and pick fights with your customers and still keep a job."

Jack dropped to one knee and cautiously helped with the cleanup. "So the boys blamed your dad for losing their dad since your dad had given him the work to do in the first place."

She offered him a thankful smile. "Exactly. When they came back home, Dad had his business going, and they insisted he owed them a job, but of course, my dad turned them down. They vowed to get even, so they sold every bit of property they had left except for the small plot under their home, and now they're trying to open a base station of their own."

"Hailey, this is crazy."

"I know. But I'm telling you, you don't have to worry about them. I don't see how they'll pass inspection, anyway." Her eyes carefully canvassed the ground for any stray slivers of glass that may have escaped their notice. Finding none, she straightened her back.

Jack stood too, opening the passenger side door and retrieving a small trash bag from beneath the seat. He emptied the glass from his hands and then held the bag open for her. "Here, make a deposit."

She obliged, carefully transferring the sharp pieces to the plastic bag.

"So, to recap, Neal and Paul have been nothing but trouble since birth and we're not going to worry about them."

He looked doubtful. "That's not a recap. That's your personal opinion."

"Educated opinion. From a lifetime of experience with those two."

"Okay, 'educated opinion.' And you're missing the point here. Forget about them passing inspection. Don't you think they're dangerous?"

She squared her shoulders, intending to end this conversation and get back on a positive topic. "Let me put your mind at ease. Everybody knows the Watson boys start drinking about the same time their eyes open in the morning. One time they even had the nerve to try to rent one of our planes. My dad refused, of course. That added fuel to the fire, let me tell you." She dusted her hands against her jeans. "But, Jack, I've known them forever, and they're basically a lot of hot air. They've let off steam now, they've let you know they're around, so they should be fine for a while. That's the way they are." She met his gaze head on. "So that's the story."

"The abbreviated version."

For a long moment, she looked back at him. "I don't figure you need to hear anything more personal than that. Just the business end." She shrugged. She knew she'd given him all the information he needed. "You still want the job?" Before he could answer, the glint of humor returned to her attitude. "Of course you do! You'll never get bored here, that's for sure."

"You're right about that. I doubt it's ever boring around here." His jaw clenched. "But you have to understand. I left working with my own father because I'm tired of constant adversity. You made your ad sound like a little piece of Heaven. I guess maybe I was hoping for something at least a *little* boring."

She looked in the direction of the kitchen and twisted her lips in thought. "Well, I'd like to say you've come to the right place, but there may be *one* more slight, little, tiny hitch." The thought of her mom's irate face appeared before her eyes.

The look on his face was sheer disappointment.

"Don't worry." She took the small trash bag from his hand. "This hitch I can certainly handle."

• • •

The look on Rinnie Holman's face when Hailey relayed the news was a mix between disbelief and fury. She dropped the paring knife along with the carrot she was slicing into the sink. "You hired him? Just like that?"

"I offered him the job, yes. I think he likes us." Hailey didn't mention anything about the Neal and Paul incident in the driveway. "He's fine. He has great references. He's a good guy, I can tell. And a hard worker. He loves the Lord. And he loves his mom. What else do we need?"

Her mom let out a snort. "He said that 'I love the Lord and I love my mom.' He said that. Those exact words."

"Not in actual out loud words, no. But it's not hard to tell what kind of person he is."

"After talking to him for thirty minutes." Her mom's outrage seemed to be bouncing off the kitchen walls. "And you put him in the cottage?"

"Mom, he has to have a place to stay for a few days. We can't expect him to find a place in town the first night he's here, can we?" She patted her mother's forearm. "Stop worrying, it'll be fine, you'll see. It's temporary. Just give the guy a chance to find a decent place in town. I know without a doubt that this is the right thing to do."

"And I know it's not," her mother insisted, with an equal amount of determination, clutching her apron with wet hands. "Put a stop to this, Hailey. Now!"

"Come on, Mom, you're getting your blood pressure up for nothing." She circled her mom in her arms, offering an affectionate hug. "You'll get used to the idea and realize that as usual, I'm right," she teased, offering a silent prayer. *Okay, Lord, it's all about You and Dad. Soften her heart, please.*

Her mother's stiff body wiggled from Hailey's grasp, returning her attention to the vegetables with sharp agitation. "We'll just see about that."

Something in her mom's tone sent a warning flag to Hailey's weary brain. "Now mom, you're not going to fly off the handle like you did that time about poor Chester, are you?" The memory of her mother, letting loose with an earsplitting scream, chasing that poor little goat around the house with a broom, flashed through her mind. It was traumatic for the entire family, but especially for Chester.

"I'm going to have a talk with Mr. What's His Name, and we'll straighten this mess out once and for all. You're not reopening this business, and that's final." Her mother turned from the sink and stepped toward the back door, tugging and fumbling with the strings on her apron in an angry effort to remove it from her waist. "And we're not having a total stranger living fifty feet from our back door, and *that's* final."

"It's fifty *yards*." Hailey plucked a fresh ripe tomato from the countertop and stepped between her mother and the door. She held the tomato in the air. "Don't make me use this, Mom."

"I'm in no mood, Hailey, and you'd best get out of my way. Now."

Hailey made moves at her mom as if she planned to launch the squishy red weapon at her. "Come on, Mom, be in the mood."

This was how her dad had always smoothed her mom's ruffled feathers. Why wasn't it working for her?

Rinnie Holman slapped the tomato from her oldest daughter's hand. It fell with a splat. Tomato seeds and juice covered the otherwise spotless floor. "Now look what you've done." The words radiated at Hailey, and neither woman made a move to clean the mess.

Hailey's teasing instantly vanished. Her heart dropped. This was more serious than she thought. And more serious than she wanted it to be. "I'm sorry, Mom. I was only trying to…" She stopped herself. She was going to admit that she was only trying to do what Dad would have done. But, admittedly, maybe she was trying too hard. Maybe she was pushing her mom too quickly. Her throat tried to close up and she swallowed hard.

She certainly didn't want to make her mom this upset.

"I don't mean any disrespect to you, Mom. I love you so much."

"I love you, too, Hailey. Yet you do what you absolutely well please regardless of how I feel or what I want."

Hailey ripped a few paper towels from the roll attached under the cabinet and stooped to scoop squashed tomato from the floor. "I'll go talk to him myself. But I'll be honest with you, Mom." She stopped to look up at her mother. "I won't tell him to leave, but I will tell him how you feel. I love you dearly, but I have to do this. It's what I'm meant…"

"There you go again with that," her mom shot back at her. "You sound like a blasted broken record. You *have* to do what you're *meant* to do."

Hailey's heart ached. She rose to her feet and stepped to the trashcan to drop the soggy wad of paper towels. She *felt* like a broken record sometimes. She felt like a broken *something* every time her and her mom went at it. *All I want to do is help mend this family. All I want to do is keep us together and afloat. All I want is for my dad to be here.*

As the door closed behind her, Hailey heard the angry tones of her mom's voice calling after her daughter. "You're meant to break your mother's heart? That's what you're *meant* to do?"

The words jabbed at her own heart. "No, Mom," she whispered, stepping out onto the yellow brick road. "But I am meant to carry on. And so are you."

Her thoughts fled to the One she knew she could turn to. *Oh, Lord, please. Reason with her. Put it in her heart to understand. I know I keep asking You. I have to trust You.*

Hailey continued on the path leading her to the other side of the hangar and to the cottage, where Jack Stinson had pulled his Jeep around to unpack what he'd need for a few days.

She wasn't sure yet what she would say to him. His introduction to the Watsons didn't go so well. How would he take her mom's objections? The words will come, she reminded herself. Somehow, they always did.

She stopped in her tracks. Jack was treading the steps between his vehicle and the cottage.

The handsome lines of his face intrigued her. He had the sturdy shoulders of a linebacker. And the steady stride of a man on a mission. He seemed so perfect for her…for the business.

She gave herself a swift reminder. *I'm not going to look at this man on a personal level. I can't think of him as anything more than a colleague. An employee. A fine-looking employee…*Sigh. *Lord, help us, please.* As she approached the Jeep, Jack looked her way and hoisted a bag of hanging clothes over a shoulder. "Well, Miss Holman," was the extent of his greeting.

Her nod his way was slow and thoughtful. "Well, Mr. Stinson." She attempted a genuine smile, but right now her lips feel heavy. *I will not look at his eyes.* This might be a bit more difficult than she thought.

First thing, she would take care of the damage done to his vehicle. And then she'd dig deep into her soul and insist that they get down to business. Putting in place her and dad's safety policies and procedures first and foremost. Then making sure the Skycat IV is air worthy. The sooner the business reopened, the sooner her mom would work through the process of accepting it. It would be the best therapy for all of them. The same as it always has been for Hailey.

CHAPTER FIVE

Hailey patted the Jeep's rear end. "I'll have this taken care of for you, Jack."

He threw her what he hoped was a no-nonsense look. "No need."

"Yes, need. First thing tomorrow, after I get you started working." She flashed him a "See, everything's going to be fine" smile. "It's the least I can do."

"I said no. But thank you. That's not necessary." He repeated a bit firmer, transferring the bag from his shoulder to hang over his forearm.

"I said I'll take care of it and I insist."

He stiffened his back and observed her with a stern eye. *Stubborn woman.* "Are you always this bull-headed?"

"Apparently." She offered him a jovial smile, but he didn't return the favor. "Okay, maybe. Yes, guilty. Bull-headed. But only when I feel strongly about something. Shouldn't we all stand firm on things we believe in?"

"I've always thought so," he conceded. "But there's a difference between standing firm and being just plain stubborn." Stubborn woman, he repeated to himself.

"Good. We're on the same page." She moistened her lips and pushed a wisp of hair behind her ear, as if the matter was perfectly settled. "Because I have something else to talk to you about."

"Don't tell me," his voice was flat. "The Watson boys are back."

"No. Of course not. Nothing that…simple. Besides, you would have heard Kisses tearing down the curtains by now if they were back."

He eyed her in tight-lipped silence as she continued.

"This is about my mom." She scratched her ear. And watched a sparrow flit from one electric pole to the next. "She's not exactly thrilled with the idea of my reopening the business."

He didn't hesitate. "That seems to be a universal consensus around here." His stare lingered on her face, waiting for the next bombshell. "I'm beginning to wonder why, exactly."

"Maybe it's the enemy."

Enemy. Was she kidding?

"You don't believe me?"

"Yah, you have enemies alright. At least two that I know of. Plus a mother with a serious problem, from what you're telling me. You might as well go ahead and spill. How many more enemies are there?" He braced himself.

The reluctance in her eyes made his stomach sink. Who was he kidding? He was about a step and a half out of here already, so if she had more, what did it matter? Tomorrow, after a good night's sleep ...

"It does seem like we have some obstacles. But they're not deal breakers," she insisted.

"No? What *would* constitute a deal breaker to you? The earth opening up and swallowing that whole hangar over there?" He jerked his head toward the metal building.

"Maybe." She shrugged. "Ya gotta know the difference between a deal breaker and a challenge."

"I want to know what I'm up against here. Just tell me," he said tiredly.

"I can sure understand that. And I'm sorry. Since you got here it's been...trying."

Trying? He rubbed the back of his neck. *No, it's been crazy.*

She took his cue. "Look, you've had a long day. We all have. Go on in and relax. Tomorrow's going to look different, I promise.

Don't worry about Neal and Paul. I'll get that light fixed tomorrow. And don't be concerned about my mom...."

"I said, I'll take care of the light." Jack undraped the garment bag from his arm and rested it on the hood, crossing his arms over his chest. "Don't evade the subject. Right now I want to hear your mother's concerns about this business."

"I'm not evading anything. Okay, yes, I can't lie. I'm evading. But we can't discuss the car later. I have to settle it now."

"Look, Hailey. Ms. Holman. I'm exhausted. I want to shower and relax. Now, please. Tell me what you need to tell me about your mom."

"Okay, then. Since you're too tired and grumpy to be reasonable, we'll discuss the light later. And I'll give you the short version of my mother's objections. That is, unless you'd like the seven-hour version, and in that case..."

"Another short version. Give me," he let out a sigh, "the short version."

"Good choice. Because there really is a long and short version to every situation."

Silence. Glare. It was his only choice to move this conversation along.

"Alright, alright, I don't have time to go into the life history of my mom and her endless list of objections to the way I've turned out, so in the interest of time..."

"Just give me the short version, *please*," he interrupted. "Give me any version." He leaned against the Jeep with a weary thud.

She took in a deep breath. "All right. The short version." She smiled. "My mom's always hated our love for flying, and she doesn't think I can handle running the business on my own. Which, I won't be on my own, since I have you."

He returned her wide smile with more deadpan silence.

Hailey continued. "She refuses to recognize the fact I helped my father run this business before I left for college. She hated it then, she hates it now. My dad trusted me to take care of things. Why can't she?"

He didn't bother to hide his annoyance. "Maybe she just wants to make sure you're not in over your head. That's not an unreasonable thought, you know."

"It's more than that. And don't defend her. You don't know the situation."

"Just like I didn't know the situation with the Watsons. If I'm going to put my reputation on the line, then I need to know what I'm getting into."

A look of determination replaced annoyance on her face. "It's flying. My mom hates anything to do with flying. She's obsessed with hating it."

He raised himself to stand upright. *This is getting more complicated by the minute.* "Is that how your father…" His voice trailed off.

"No. Flying was my dad's life." She met his eyes boldly. "Flying had nothing to do with his death." Mist stung her eyes but she worked to hold it in check. "He had a heart attack."

He hesitated. "I can see how the business could stir up painful memories for her. Can't you?"

"Why are you defending her again? She has to face the memories head on, every memory, like we all have. Then she can get past that pain and remember the joy again. She knows how much flying meant to my dad. And she insists that I give it up even though she knows how much it's always meant to us. She just wants to control me, that's all. Why can't she be thankful we still have something left that was so much a part of Dad?"

He stiffened. If anyone knew anything about trying to be controlled, it was him. And her mom might be a little insistent, but controlling? From what he perceived of Hailey so far, he wasn't sure anyone on earth could control her.

"Everyone's different. Cut your mother some slack. Your joy happens to be her pain. Maybe you need to sit back and show her some sensitivity. See it from her side."

"I can't believe you!" Blue eyes flared. "Why do you insist on taking her side? I'm not being insensitive. I'm *very* sensitive to how she feels. She's being stubborn. It's the one thing she couldn't control in my father. No matter what's happened in the past, I was born to fly, Jack. And she'll have to get used to it with me, just as she had to get used to it with Dad."

"Obviously, she didn't get used to it with your dad, Hailey. She may have tolerated it. And from what I'm seeing here, stubborn didn't fall far from the tree." He reached to close the Jeep door with a solid push. "Listen, I don't think this is going to work out for me. I'm here for two reasons. To do what I love, which is working on planes. And to find some sense of peace in my life. Obviously this is the wrong place for either. I'll stay here at your cottage tonight if that's okay, and be on my way tomorrow. We'll call it even. Lodging for a night in exchange for you not having the taillight fixed." He held his hand out to her. "Let's just shake on it. How's that?"

She ignored his hand. "I certainly won't hold you here, but for heaven's sake, Jack, don't let these little things scare you away."

"Little things? You have two drunken lunatics out to stop you from opening this business. They might be nuisances you're used to dealing with, but come on, I'm thinking it's bound to be a little nuts around here and since my goal is a significant lifestyle change, that's not exactly the scenario I'm looking for. And your own mom is so disturbed by what you're doing that she's throwing produce at you."

"Oh. You heard."

"Ms. Holman, I'm not sure exactly how big this county is, but I'm sure at least half of it heard. I wasn't going to mention it because I thought it might embarrass you. So your idea of 'little things,'" he air parenthesized the words, "don't compute to 'little things' in my book. This situation seems hopeless from where I stand."

She nodded. "Okay, I can see your point. Jack, I'll tell ya, when God writes a big fat N-O in the sky, then I'll say that's a big thing. Then the plans will be over."

The look he cast in her direction hopefully conveyed his skepticism.

"Seriously, Jack. But I can tell you that's not going to happen. It's my calling. I know it as sure as I know that I'm Web Holman's oldest daughter."

He squeezed the spot between his eyebrows before giving her a frustrated sigh. "I'll tell you what. I'm probably going to regret this, but I do not go back on my word." He rubbed a hand over his face and then looked her square in the eye. "I'll stay until you find another victim…I mean applicant. Or until I find another job. Whichever comes first. And then I'm gone. Agreed?"

He knew he'd won this round when she met his hand halfway with hers. Maybe this isn't the right job for him after all.

Jack watched the confident young woman make her way back along the brick walkway and into the back door of the main house.

He didn't know whether to be irritated with her or impressed. She certainly knew what she wanted, he had to give her that. He'd never met anyone like her. Whether that was good or bad was yet to be seen.

Jack moved up the steps and onto the cottage porch. He'd unloaded enough of his things to get by. At this point he really wasn't sure whether he'd be here one day or ten, but he had always been good for his word. He stopped in his tracks. *Did I just promise to stay until she finds someone else?* He groaned out loud. *I need to have my head examined.*

Walking into the living room of the well-crafted cottage, he tossed his keys onto the entry table and set his clothes and bag on the nearest chair. He surveyed the homey surroundings before sinking down on the blue and white striped sofa.

A weary sigh slipped through his lips. *What is it she kept saying? That this business was her "calling"?* He massaged his aching temples. The only calling he could remember hearing about was someone being "called" into the ministry.

Jack tossed the thoughts around in his head. It seemed so complicated. What would his calling be? What about his dad? What about those boys…those Watson boys? *We choose a path and hope it's the right one. It's our choice to make. God just makes sure we behave ourselves. He's sort of the big disciplinarian in the sky. Right?*

Jack tugged at his boots, letting them drop to the floor before falling back to stretch across the sofa. He let his eyes fall shut. Maybe he should have continued to attend church with his mother after he'd started working at the company. But who could spare the time? As it was, he'd been working seven days a week. His father had never seen the need for church. Maybe that was reason enough to have continued going with her, Jack thought wryly.

He rubbed a hand across his face again. Maybe just a quick nap, and then he'd drive into town to get something to eat. He'd try… who was that she mentioned earlier? Uncle Somebody's Diner.

Open irritation crept into his weary thoughts. At first glance he thought he'd found paradise. Now he'd have to initiate the search all over again. Her finding someone else? That could take days… weeks. *What have I gotten myself into?*

Frustration started rising from the pit of his stomach. *It's going to be another Tylenol popping day after all. Just like back home.* His mind circled around the aggravations, the charts, graphs, reports—from the first day his dad stuck him in the office, he'd wanted out.

"Stinsons start at the top. Not in the grease pit with the hired help"' His father's words.

But his father's idea of the top wasn't where Jack wanted to be. He wanted to work with his hands. Be with the people who made it all happen. He wanted to accomplish something important to him. Marshall Stinson's impatience for Jack's resistance to run the business as a big time conglomerate made for constant friction in the office. Jack knew it only hindered productivity. And even worse, kept the wedge between father and son growing.

He stood and headed toward his bag.

Not exactly the grand escape he'd planned.

CHAPTER SIX

"That's crazy! Why would you want to drive all the way into town to eat when we have a perfectly good meal sitting on the table waiting for you right now?" Hailey stood at the cottage door, her hands thrust on her hips.

Jack graciously declined her invitation for a second time. "I've already made plans to drive into town to eat. And I have phone calls to make."

"Jack, you don't know anybody around here to make plans with."

"Who said making plans constituted the need for two or more parties? I made plans with myself to do this, and that's what I'm going to do."

She pointed through the open door to the telephone sitting on the oak table beside the sofa. "And if you don't want to use your cell phone, there's a perfectly good phone right there, Mr. Smarty. Walk to the house and eat. I promise you won't be forced to have social hour with us. Just eat and then walk right straight back here and use that phone."

"No. But thank you."

"You know, I can see why you feel uncomfortable." An understanding smile tipped her lips. "But I know once my mom meets you, she'll start warming to the situation. You'll win her over with your sparkling wit." She sucked in a breath and waited for his reply. That might have come out wrong, she warned herself. "You know I was teasing, right? Not that you're not witty. I'm not saying you're completely without wit." *Okay, Hailey. Stop.*

"You're not being realistic, Hailey. You think just because your mom meets me, she'll be swept off her feet and reconsider her position on flying and your plans?"

Not offended. Good. Because she really was only teasing. Hailey shrugged, turning up her smile a notch. "You are 'feet sweeping off of' material." She felt her face flush.

"I can't, in good conscience, antagonize your mother that way. She doesn't need me at her table. And what are you doing? Trying to butter me up? I don't butter easily."

"All right. I do understand." She saw his eyes narrow. "I guess I'll see you at the hangar in the morning, then. Seven sharp." She smiled at him with what she hoped showed no trace of disappointment and turned to make her way down the steps.

"Wait."

She turned to face him, her eyebrows questioning his command.

"Tell me how to get to your uncle's diner."

"It's on the main drag right through Barnes. Believe me, you can't miss it. Of course, they close at two-thirty so you'd better get a move on if you're going." She tapped her watch. "One-forty right now. Thirty minute drive. Did I mention it's the only restaurant in town?" She smoothed a nonexistent wrinkle in her work shirt. "Or I could always bring you over a nice quick plate of hot food. Chicken and wild rice. Fresh vegetables. Hot buttered rolls."

She could tell he was reconsidering the offer by the serious scowl on his face.

"Okay," he relented. "But only because fresh hot buttered rolls are a weakness of mine. I don't want to make things more difficult for your family."

"You're not," she assured him. "I'll be back in two minutes with your plate." She bopped down the steps.

"Thanks," he called after her and closed the door.

• • •

It was no great surprise to him that she was already at the hangar at six forty-five the next morning. The hangar doors were thrown open on both sides, the early morning April sun starting to stream through, highlighting her frame engulfed in clouds of dust as she pushed a broom with intense strokes around the concrete floor. Kisses lay stretched out in the doorway, oblivious to the dust storm swirling around him.

Maybe he could walk, invisibly, past her and get his hands on those two beautiful Skycats parked on the other end of the hangar.

No such luck. Hailey noticed him as she stopped sweeping to bite off a piece of chocolate bar.

He smiled in greeting and stopped to stroke Kisses's big head.

The dog's heavy tail thumped firmly against the cement.

"Candy for breakfast?" He eyed the bar she dropped back into her work shirt pocket.

"Not usually." The exaggerated scowl on her face turned into a mild grin. "My mom and I got into it already this morning. I know I shouldn't let it get to me, but it does. I hate it, in fact."

His hands were on his hips. "Still think it'll all work out?"

"Oh, sure." She moved across the floor to prop the broom beside a meticulous wooden workbench spanning the length of one entire wall. "She'll come around." Her usual teasing glint returned. "You'll probably want to stick around to see how nicely it all works out."

He chose to ignore the optimistic remark.

She kept smiling. "Okay, so you're not up for a rousing verbal swap this morning. That's fine. Want to check out the planes?"

The sparkle in her eye was contagious. He was more than anxious to get his hands on those planes.

He followed closely as she made brisk strides to stand beside the aircraft.

"Beauties, aren't they?" Love for the planes was evident in her voice. She seemed to observe his reaction proudly, her hands stuck into the pockets of her jeans.

Jack conducted a brief examination, reveling in the prospect of getting his hands as greasy as possible.

Temporarily, of course. Since he was on a job search again.

"Well, what do you think? Can you help get 'em ready for some air time?"

He walked to the rear of the plane. "From what I can tell without an internal check, this rudder is about the worst of it. Just basic maintenance, really."

She followed him around to the other side of the plane. Approaching the door he halted, reading the words inscribed with perfect script lettering: "Hailey's Comet." He shot her an admiring glance. "Clever. I like it."

She leaned against the fuselage, patting the side of the Skycat III with loving hands. "Jack, meet Comet. Comet, this is Jack."

"Hailey's Comet," he repeated. "That really is clever."

"That's my dad for you." She bent to run a hand along the bottom of the Skycat where she'd previously sanded. "Well, are you going to stand around wasting time, or are you gonna get to work?"

He stopped admiring the craft long enough to shoot her a wary look. "You don't give up, do you?"

"That's what got me where I am today, Mr. Stinson." She teased.

He fought the urge to grin. Where she was today, it appeared to him, was swimming upstream without a paddle.

He thrust his hands on his hips and let an exaggerated scowl cross his face. "I suppose I could piddle around here today. Nothing else to do in this one-horse town."

She was obviously pleased. "Well come ooh-and-aahh over our tools, then." Before the words left her mouth, she was already halfway back to the workbench.

He made his way over. "This really is a very nice operation you have here."

"Thanks. You wouldn't believe how much thought Dad put into everything. I'm going to leave everything exactly the way it was the day he left it."

"Are you certain about that?" he asked with a frown.

"Why, yes." Her surprise was visible. "What do you think is wrong with it?"

His eyes scanned the premises for an example. "Now, here. This is what I mean." He walked to the far end of the workbench. "If the plane is going to come in facing north," he stood facing the same direction as the nose of the plane, holding his arms out straight in front of him for emphasis, "I would have built the tool racks on this end so I wouldn't have to walk around the tail and wings each time I needed something."

He continued, crossing the cement floor and sweeping his arms across the room. "And I would have had the entry poured on the north side of the structure as well as the south side, because if I needed to change the direction I brought the plane in, say for wind direction purposes, my options wouldn't be limited to one entrance. It's smart for fire safety, too."

He was about to give his reasons for portable instead of stationary chocks, but he caught a glimpse of her face and thought better of it. He blinked at her. "What? What's wrong?"

She looked as if the breath had been knocked out of her. "Nothing. I know you weren't criticizing, but my dad planned this out so carefully."

Had he hurt her feelings? He hoped not. Poor girl was going through enough already. "I've already told you I think this is an incredible operation."

He moved quickly to stand beside her. "I didn't mean to sound overly critical." He berated himself for not realizing how his immediate suggestions might sound to her. It had been only six months since she lost her father. And though she appeared to be handling the loss exceptionally well, he had to wonder.

He offered her an awkward pat on the shoulder.

She took a deep breath, giving the hangar a tender glance. "My dad was quite a perfectionist."

"It shows." He assessed the neatly labeled drawers of nuts and bolts. "I have a dose of it, myself. Perfectionism. So does my own father."

"I learned a great deal about doing things right from my dad." Her eyes glistened.

He wished he could say the same about his own dad, but he couldn't. "My father thought his way was the only right way. His way was to hold his thumb over anyone who had ideas or dreams of their own." He turned away from the workbench and faced the aircraft. "I don't think that's the right way."

Her blue eyes regained a little spark. "Oh! So you *don't* think it's okay for *your* father to keep you from doing what *you* think you should do, but it *is* okay for *my* mom to try to do the same thing to *me?*"

Ouch. "Look, you don't understand the situation," he insisted.

"I understand it perfectly. It's the same old double standard."

"Double standard?" He was taken aback. "How? Our situations aren't the same at all. My father was controlling."

"And my mom isn't trying to control me? Oh, that's right. You decided that after five minutes yesterday." Her voice held no anger. But she was certainly up for a debate, judging by her stance. "Come on, Jack. Admit it. I have every bit as much right to pursue my calling as you do."

Her words cut through him. That calling again. "Your mother isn't unreasonable like my father is."

She let out an astonished gasp. "You don't know unreasonable until you've tried to talk some sense into Rinnie Holman."

She stood before him, hands perched on her hips, he supposed expecting a rebuttal.

For a split second he forgot he wanted to argue with her. All he saw was how beautiful her determination and strength made her. He always thought his mother was the strongest woman he'd ever known. But her strength was quiet and tolerant. Hailey's was questioning and bold. She was filled with a vibrant strength too impressive to ignore.

"Listen, Hailey, if I wanted to argue I could have stayed in Cryder working for my father. I've told you I made this change because I want peace and quiet in my life. Let's make the short time I have here as pleasant as possible."

"One, this isn't Cryder, Jack. And two, we can disagree without making a federal case of it. That's what I can't get my mom to understand, either. I don't *like* to argue!"

Before he could respond, she continued. "Why don't you put more thought into staying here? You obviously love the planes. And believe it or not, this can be the most tranquil place you'll find. Sure, once in awhile things get crazy, like yesterday with Neal and Paul and this thing with my mom, but hang around and you'll find that this is exactly what you're looking for. Any place you go will have something about it you don't like. And not to sound selfish, but with your experience, you're exactly what I'm looking for. This could be exactly what both of us need."

"You're forgetting, I've been stuck in administration for so long that I'm rusty at working with my hands." He wanted her to see a negative to him staying. Even if he really didn't believe it himself. "I've barely hung on to my A & P certification."

"That's not a big deal at all. You'll get your hours in no time. In fact, your business knowledge will be a real asset as the Wild Blue Yonder Flyers grows."

The thought instantly agitated him. She wanted to take what her dad started and *grow* it? That defeated the purpose of having a family business—that's when it could become something no one even recognizes anymore. "If you start talking that way, you're going to ruin a potentially good thing. The beauty of this business is its simplicity. Keep it that way."

"You're saying start small and stay small?" Her voice rang through the metal building. "That's not what my dad had in mind! I'm not talking about anything as humongous as what you're used to. But there's a huge need for what we do around here. We may have been a small time operation to you, Mr. Stinson, but our dreams are anything but small."

Her lecture was halted by the intrusive roar of a now-familiar mufflerless pickup careening up the driveway, spewing gravel and dust in its wake. Before the oversized tires could come to a skidding stop at the hangar door, Kisses was on his feet, ready to lunge at the truck's two loud occupants. The hair along the ridge of the dog's back stood like the bristles of a porcupine, his bark enraged and ferocious, his teeth bared and ready.

Jack wanted to bare his teeth, too.

The driver spit through the open window, seemingly unperturbed at the dog's threat. "Well, lookee. Miz Hailey has 'erself a li'l helper."

Hailey raked a determined hand through her bangs. "Paul Watson, I strongly suggest you get off my property." Her voice was steady.

The man behind the steering wheel let out a loud whoop as he cut the motor. "Lordy, you are lookin' so fine to-day, missy." He muttered something to the person in the passenger side of the truck and both men cackled.

Paul leaned his face out the window. "Neal says you're lookin' mighty fine, too, Hailey girl."

It didn't take the stench of alcohol drifting from the truck to know that the two were polluted. And it was barely eight A.M.

Jack felt the blood rush to the top of his head as he took a step forward. "You heard the lady," he issued with a thread of warning. "Get off her property."

Paul smiled and tipped the brim of his cap back with the rim of the beer bottle in his hand. "Well, now, city boy. We got ourselves a li'l problem, there. This gal thinks she's gonna mess us over again."

His crooked grin revealed tobacco-stained teeth. "But she ain't." He reached his hand around to the outside of his truck, fumbling with the door handle.

Kisses let out a vicious warning growl, and Paul snapped his hand back. "I hate that no sood, gorry hound." Paul and Neal both threw their heads back in a fit of laughter at Paul's slurred words. "I mean that no good, sorry hound." He spit a stream of nasty tobacco toward the dog.

Kisses didn't flinch but held his dark eyes riveted on Paul and Neal. Jack had no doubt the dog was ready and capable of defending his master at the slightest command. It wouldn't take much. It was obvious that Kisses felt the same way about the Watson brothers as they felt about him.

"Aw, never min' that, Paul," Neal spoke up. "Tell 'er she ain't gonna reopen this place no how, no way."

Paul gave a firm nod and tipped his head toward his brother. "Yeah. Whut he said."

Jack had been prepared to take his cue from Hailey, but now he could no longer hold his tongue. The hair on the back of his neck stood up, just about the way Kisses's did. They weren't going to treat her this way. He'd put an end to this nonsense once and for all.

He took long strides until he stood less than a foot from the truck. "Now, you boys listen, and you listen good—"

Before he could continue, she was beside him. "Thanks, Jack, but I know how to handle these two." Her eyes never left their faces. She spoke sternly as if reprimanding small, naughty children. "Neal. Paul. You've been warned. The only time you are welcome here is when you're sober." She lowered her voice and muttered under her breath. "In other words, never."

"Come on, sweet thang." Neal's voice reeked of sarcasm. "You know we kin do lots better if we work together on this thang. Yur gonna be takin' bread outta li'l Dee's mouth. And Mama's. Now, ya don't want that, do ya, suga' plum?"

She crossed her arms. "For what you spend on beer in two days, you could feed the four of ya'll for two months. Carleen and Dee won't go hungry, we'll always see to that. But you two," she gave them a piercing look, "you're on your own. Now get out of here and stay out. The Blue Yonder Flyers will open as planned."

She turned on her heel to walk back into the hangar, followed closely by her faithful dog.

Jack waited until the two had revved the engine and fled the premises. The obscenities hurled through their windows stirred up more than just the dust and gravel from their tires. He watched them until they were out of sight and the roar of the old truck no longer filled the air. Then he turned his attention back to the courageous young woman who knelt on one knee, her back to him, stroking the big dog's head.

"You really stood up to those two out there. I'm really impressed. But maybe you'd get some resolution to this if you'd let me handle it man to man."

"Uh, yeah, well, that's not happening." She stood to face him. "You're expecting way too much from those two. Man to man? *Please.*"

Hailey walked back toward the open doors and stood without a word.

Jack wasn't sure whether to get back to work or go to her side. He gave her some space, then finally took steps to stand beside her. "Thinking about the Watson's?"

She turned her attention his way. "I was just thinking how everything got started. I can remember my dad sitting at the dining room table with his big drafting sheets, drawing out plans for the hangar. And my mom standing beside him, telling him what an impossible and foolish dream it was. Sort of like the way she does now with me." Hailey's voice held a sadness that touched him.

"I can only imagine what you're feeling right now, Hailey."

"Well, if you can imagine how infuriating those Watson boys are to me, then yes, you know how I feel. They try to ruin everything."

"And admirably, you're determined not to let them."

"Would you?" Her eyes scanned his face.

He had to admit. No, he would not.

"If it weren't for the booze and bad tempers, they'd still have their crop dusting business. I can't stand the thought of anyone needing a plane around here and being at the mercy of those two bullies. It's like I always told my dad, they'd sell their own mother for pure meanness."

"Can't say I doubt you're right."

"And now poor Ms. Carleen has Neal's six-year-old daughter, Dee, to raise."

"Scary thought. That guy reproducing." He didn't mean it as a slam, but the thought really was unsettling.

"I wish I could disagree. But none of us can imagine life without that little girl. Neal married a girl from Cypress County when she was about a month from giving birth to their daughter. Ms. Carleen took them in, fed them, and made sure mother and baby had health care. Within three months, the girl ran off with a welder from Greensville. Nice, huh?"

"That's rough."

"It just doesn't seem fair that Ms. Carleen is stuck with so much to deal with on her own. We know we weren't responsible for Mr.

Watson's death, but we'll be here for Carleen and Dee forever. We love those girls, but something serious has to be done about Neal and Paul. It's so unfair." Hailey let a weary sigh leave her lips and the conversation lapsed for a minute. She picked up a wrench and flipped it end over end and heaved another deep sigh.

Her shoulders rose and fell quickly as she set the wrench back down and picked up the bag she'd tossed on the workbench earlier. She held it open for him to inspect.

"Your chocolates are melted." He announced.

The look she tossed him was unconcerned. "If you hang around us Holman's long enough, you'll find that there's no problem we can't solve."

"Is that what you were doing just now, lost in thought, solving problems?"

She jerked open a drawer and retrieved a zipped baggy full of plastic spoons and forks. Dipping her hand in, she seized a spoon and waved it through the air. Her eyes narrowed. "That's exactly what I was doing. Solving problems." She dipped a spoonful of melted chocolate. "Now. What were we arguing about before we were so crudely interrupted?"

Everything. That's what he wanted to say. But he knew arguing wasn't really the word for what they were doing. This woman had a way of holding his attention and making it hard for him not to smile. Even when she was being infuriatingly hardheaded.

He avoided looking into her intriguing eyes. "Okay, so what do you think they'll do next? The Watson brothers, I mean."

"Stay passed out for a week, maybe. Who knows with those two. But don't worry about it, Jack. God can handle them. Same way He's gonna change my mom's heart."

A nagging doubt tugged at his mind. Sure, God *could* do it. Or so he had heard. But *would* He? It seemed to him that God chose to work His miracles rather sparingly. How many years had his mother prayed that his father would change his angry ways and go to church with her? And stop being such a tyrant to his family and employees? It hadn't happened and didn't look promising.

Obviously, the Stinson family wasn't on God's priority list, or He would have worked things out for his family.

He watched her dip into the bag of chocolate again. *Whether she'll admit it or not, Hailey's situation is so different with her mother than what we faced with my father.*

Why does she think she's so different? Why would God listen to her and not to me or my mother? At least her mother isn't forcing her to go against her principles. I'll never condone some of my father's business practices. Things like learning ahead of time what a competitor bid on a project and then underbidding just enough to land the job. And making a promise on a deadline with no intention of keeping it. I've always tried to do the right thing. The honest thing. But it certainly hasn't gotten us anywhere with God.

So he had to wonder again: *Why does she think she's so different?*

Hailey wiped a smudge of chocolate from her lips. "Jack, God only knows what those two will do next, or when Mom will come to her senses. I only know what I have to do. And what I'm going to do." She threw the empty chocolate bag and wrappings, along with the plastic spoon, into a nearby trashcan and rested her hands on her hips. "I'm getting on with my duties. There's a bunch of work to do." She cocked her head to the side and eyed him boldly. "Are you with me, or not?"

He studied her face before nodding and turning his attention to work.

"Good." She slipped a rubber band from her wrist and wrapped it around her hair into a neck skimming ponytail. "Now, where were we? We've wasted enough time on the Watsons."

While his hands got busy surveying one of the planes, his mind couldn't stay completely on task. Was he with her or not? Actually, he wanted to know the same thing. *Man, she makes it hard to walk away.*

He could identify with Hailey in a lot of ways. She believed in what she was doing, regardless of what others said. She wasn't arrogant about it or overly pushy. Well, maybe pushy. He stifled a grin. But her determination was contagious. And her down-to-earth boldness—certainly attractive.

Neal and Paul Watson didn't bother him nearly as much as the realization that he'd have to meet face to face with Mrs. Holman at some point. He didn't relish the thought of being where he wasn't wanted. Personal or not. Maybe if he left, Hailey wouldn't be able to find someone else and she'd give up.

He almost laughed out loud. *That's a ludicrous thought.* After knowing her for less than one day, he knew better. She'd somehow handle the whole thing by herself if she had to, he was certain of it.

Maybe he could help Hailey and her mom arrive at some kind of compromise. Maybe he could actually do some good around here with his negotiation skills.

His eyes searched the determined face before him. Deep into her work, the flame in her sky blue eyes burned bright. And the fixed resolution of her voice when she spoke gave her an invincible air. But he sensed a vulnerability. A vulnerability that he already knew she'd never readily admit to.

CHAPTER SEVEN

"So what's it gonna be, Mr. Stinson?" An hour later and there was no doubt in Hailey's mind that Jack had been contemplating her question as he mapped some wiring inside one of the planes. Nobody worked as intensely as he'd been without being pretty excited about it. This job was perfect for him and she knew it. Surely he knew it, too.

She met his eyes boldly. "You know you want to stay. Admit it."

"I never said I didn't *want* to."

She checked her watch. "It's almost ten already." She reached for a package of fine grade sandpaper hanging on the wall. "I'll finish the rust spots I started yesterday, and you can start working on the elevator."

She began sanding on the plane as her mind took off on a bittersweet journey of its own. *This is my domain,* Hailey thought with a surge of tenderness. *Mine and Dad's.*

His death left a void in her heart that she was certain no one could ever fill. She knew her mom to be a devoted and able parent, but Hailey couldn't help but feel that she, herself, was now responsible for the family.

"There are two kinds of folks on this earth," Web Holman always said. "Those who stand below staring up into God's great heavens, and those who soar smack dab into those great heavens."

That's how she learned to approach everything, soaring smack dab, full speed ahead.

Out of the corner of her eye she was suddenly aware of Jack watching her. She gave him her full attention, as one corner of his mouth twisted upward. "What?" She always seemed to want to smile at him.

"I suppose I might as well do something constructive while I'm here," he announced, as if she thought he'd do any different.

She flashed him a triumphant smile. "My sentiments exactly."

Three hours later, Jack stood beside the workbench scrubbing at his hands with a towel. "I can definitely get into this kind of work."

"Well, degrease yourself and let's go in for lunch before my mom changes her mind about feeding us."

He stopped scrubbing and looked at her. "If that's an invitation to have lunch with you and your family, I appreciate it," he shook his head, "but no, thanks. I think we've definitely ruled out me sitting at the same table with your mom any time soon, if ever. I'll run into town. Your uncle's diner sounds really good about now."

She shook her head. "Absolutely not. Home-cooked meals are just one of the many perks you'll get working here at The Blue Yonder Flyers. Besides, it'll take thirty minutes to drive all the way into town. That's sixty minutes of drive time. And don't forget, this is the busiest...."

"...time of day at the diner," he finished her sentence. "I don't mind. I need to get a few groceries anyway. I'm perfectly capable of cooking for myself while I'm here."

Her lips turned up in a mischievous smile. "What? You cook? I figured you for more of a dress for dinner and be served in the grand dining hall kind of guy."

He snorted. "You make me sound like a snob. I'm not going to make things any more uncomfortable for your poor mother than they already are."

"My poor mom?" Her brows drew together in a questioning frown. "You'll have to get over feeling sorry for my mom, Jack.

She's been given every opportunity to be a part of the business when it was my father and I. She has the same opportunity now, if she wants."

She was tempted to add: "This-is-a-recording. My-mother-will-accept-the-business. This-is-a-recording."

Jack gave her a doubtful look. "Yes, ma'am. Whatever you say."

"All you have to do is your job, and I'll do mine."

"I understand, but while I'm here, maybe I can help the situation with your mom. I've had to unruffle my share of irritated customers and employees. Thanks to my dad," he added. "If there's one thing I've learned about business, it's that direct communication is the key."

"Direct communication?" She patted the side of her leg to summon Kisses from his place lying in the sunny doorway. She cocked her head at him, stifling a knowing grin. "My dad tried that for years. And if you think my problems are hopeless, you sure don't know what can happen when God's on your side."

She gave Kisses a tousle on the head. "And that, Mr. Stinson, is about as direct as a person can get in the communication department. Now let's go eat. I'm starving!"

• • •

To say that lunchtime was awkward would be a gross understatement. Jack decided he'd have to give Hailey's mom credit. Rinnie Holman was the epitome of graciousness. Detached graciousness, but graciousness nonetheless.

Something about her reminded him of his own mom, except for the fact that Hailey was right: his own mother would have served an elegant luncheon in the formal dining room. Under different circumstances, he would have preferred this more casual meal around the kitchen table to the stiff dinner time rituals his dad insisted on. Everyone, and that meant every member of the family, was not only expected but required to sit at the massive mahogany table until Marshall finished his last bite and scooted his chair from the table. Meals were exhausting at his house. And usually quiet. With the exception of some sporadic business talk initiated by his dad. Or some critical analysis of something Jack had done. Or not done.

Jack dropped those thoughts and turned them instead to his mother. Now with his younger brother gone to Virginia Tech on a football scholarship, she was alone with his dad. If Hailey could see what his mother went through to keep the peace around their home, she might realize her mom wasn't really that bad. Disagreeable maybe, but not bad.

What could have happened to Marshall Stinson during his life to make him so hard to deal with? He'd always been what Jack considered overly strict, but with every passing year, his irrational demands seemed to grow worse.

Jack placed his napkin on the table and pushed his chair back. "Thank you, Mrs. Holman, I appreciate lunch. It was delicious."

Rinnie Holman's dark eyes never left the table as she scooped up the basket of leftover rolls. "You are welcome, Mr. Stinson. And thank you," she said, her voice edged with formality.

Jack reached for his plate, but the older woman whisked it from his hands without a word.

Hailey had excused herself to answer the phone, and he found himself hoping she wouldn't return too quickly. He intended to have a talk with Mrs. Holman. By himself. He wanted to hear her side. There had to be more to this than even Hailey knew, and he didn't mind being the negotiator. That was something he was actually really good at. He'd hate to see an inoperable rift tear this family apart. The way it appeared his own family had been torn.

Someone had to give Hailey a reality check about what was going on with her mom. It might as well be him.

"Mrs. Holman, Hailey tells me that you're not happy about her plans to reopen the business. I'd like to hear your objections. Maybe I can help in some way."

Rinnie turned from the sink and faced him squarely, her hands still wet from rinsing food from the dishes. "Mr. Stinson, at this point I have no quarrel with you personally. This matter is between my daughter and myself. She's pig-headed and wants her own way in this, just as her father did. I had no control over him. But I should have at least a little bit over her."

"I honestly don't think this is about her wanting control, Mrs. Holman. If you have a viable reason for not wanting Hailey to fly or to reopen the business, can you talk to her about it? Maybe the two of you could come to some sort of—"

"Compromise? Is that what you're getting at, Mr. Stinson?"

"Yes. A compromise. No harm can come from discussing your concerns."

"My 'concerns,' Mr. Stinson, are none of your business." Her eyes burned through him.

He took a step closer to her. She certainly seems closed. But Jack was used to tough customers. "Mrs. Holman, I'm not here to make trouble. I promise you that. I don't even know how I got into the middle of this, but somehow I seem to be."

"That's most unfortunate, because I suppose," she turned back to her dishwater, "you're a nice enough young man. But the fact is, you are putting yourself into the middle of a great big pile of trouble. No good can come of this." She lifted the stack of plates from the counter and sloshed them into the dishwater. "No good at all."

"I promise I'm not trying to get into your personal business, Mrs. Holman."

She turned to face him. "There's more than—"

Before she could finish, Hailey breezed into the kitchen. "That was Ms. Carleen." She halted in her steps, looking at her mom.

And then at Jack. "What have you two been talking about, as if I don't already know."

Jack kept his mouth shut. Seriously. It was not his place to try to solve their problems. But here he was, standing between two feuding women.

Hailey cut the silence. "Well, good. You two are going to be swell friends, I can tell." She pushed her mom away from the sink with a playful bump of her hip. "You'd better sit while you can, Mama dear, because Dee's on her way." She handed her mom a dishcloth to dry her hands on, working with her back to Jack as she offered him more information on Dee.

"She's a handful, let me tell you. Just as precious as she can be, though."

She tossed a brief look of irritation over her shoulder. "We don't hold it against her that she's Neal Watson's daughter, right Mom?"

Her mother huffed tight-lipped from the kitchen as Hailey wrung the water from the cloth and turned to wipe the table. "Man, Jack. What did you do to my mother?"

"What did *I* do? All I did was try to talk to her," he replied.

She leaned across the table to give it one last wipe. "Well, there you go. You tried to talk to her." She let out an exaggerated sigh. "Direct communication, right? I hate to say I told you so."

"Then don't." He narrowed his eyes at her. "But I'm telling you, the woman has more against flying than she's telling. I can't help but feel that there's something else."

"Don't try to read some big mystery into this, Jack. There's no deep, dark motive lurking in the shadows here. My mom's unfounded objections are very well known." She put a hand on her hip, deep in thought. "You know, I'm beginning to think she just needs to feel like she's more a part of things. Maybe we need to find a way to get her involved so she'll feel needed."

His skepticism didn't seem to surprise her.

"Jack, I appreciate the attempt you made." Her eyes conveyed sincere appreciation. "But our job is to honor my dad's memory and continue doing his work. Mom will be okay."

"I only hope I didn't make things worse."

She shook her head and let out a little snort. "Worse? You couldn't have." Her voice was steady. She folded the washcloth and laid it across the sink, turning to face him. "Jack, listen, I know how you feel. You've been dealing with a difficult family situation of your own, and now you're thrust into someone else's difficult family situation. But I promise you, this is going to work out. God will work it out because it's what's right." She let out a deep sigh. "How many times and ways do I need to say this? I love my mom and I know she'll come to her senses. So let's just give her some more time." Her voice was firm. Final. "Trust me when I tell you that the rest will fall into place."

He drew his lips in and doubts swirled through his brain. *I'm not sure. How many times and ways* can *she say it?*

Hailey continued. "Besides, with Dee here, she won't have time to worry about what we're doing."

"Now, come on." Jack had to chuckle. "How much mischief can a six-year-old get into?"

She tossed her head back and let out a knowing laugh. "Dee Watson could dismantle the Statue of Liberty in thirty minutes. Twenty-five on a good sugar-high day. I have to hide my chocolate stash from her or she goes wild." A tender smile touched her lips. "Poor little darling, she's had it rough. It would have been nice if Neal was the kind of guy to take responsibility for a child, but what are the chances of that at this point, right?"

"It's nice that you and your family are so close to the little girl. And to Mrs. Watson."

"It's not just us. My Uncle Frank and Aunt Shirley help a lot, too. Ms. Carleen's an excellent hostess and server at the diner."

Her face brightened. "Dee loves being around the airplanes almost as much as I do."

"She won't be hanging around while we work, will she? I don't think that's safe."

"Come on, Jack. She's been around us and our planes all her life. I keep a close eye on her. She knows what she's supposed to stay away from."

"It's not a wise move, that's all I'm saying. She's a little kid. Little kids get into things. You said so yourself, she's a dismantler."

"Well, we don't have to worry about it much anyway. Between my mom and Felicia, and my middle sister Lindsey, when she's home from school, I hardly get that much time with Deedles."

The doorbell sounded and Hailey motioned with her head. "She's here. Come on, I can't wait to show her off to you."

The little girl running to Hailey with a fierce leap into her arms was followed by a weary eyed but smiling woman. That had to be Mrs. Watson.

Hailey made the introductions, but the only shred of resemblance Jack saw between Carleen Watson and her two wild sons were the deep-set eyes and high cheek bones. Nothing in the woman's demeanor would have tipped him off that she'd been the poor unfortunate human who bore those two thugs.

Mrs. Watson gave Hailey a fierce hug. "Thank you, sweetie. I'm not working late tonight. Your Uncle Frank just needed me at the last minute. The diner's hoppin' today, he says."

Jack's lips formed a knowing smile. "Busiest time of the day."

Hailey issued him a "see, told you" look.

Mrs. Watson kissed the top of her granddaughter's head and left the kitchen, heading to work. Dee was already tugging on Hailey's hand. "Come on, Hailey, let's go see the planes."

"I have a better idea. First, let's go show Mr. Stinson our swing and secret hiding place."

The little girl's light brown curls bobbed up and down. "Race ya'!"

Dee and Hailey ran all the way to the back pasture, followed by the much slower moving Jack.

When he reached them, huffing and puffing, Dee was already settled on a wooden plank, notched and set against a sturdy rope hanging from a thick-trunked china berry tree.

"You didn't…" he tried to catch his breath, pulling a handkerchief from his back pocket and wiping at the perspiration on his face. "You didn't tell me we'd be jogging halfway across the state."

"You didn't ask," Hailey teased, and Dee giggled.

"Swing me higher, higher!"

Hailey gave the little girl a giant shove. "Any higher and you'd hit your little pumpkin head on those clouds up there."

Dee let out an earsplitting squeal of delight. "*Weeeeeeeeeeeeeee!* Those clouds are *soft*! That won't hurt, Hailey!"

Jack shook the tightness from his leg muscles and surveyed the area. It actually felt good to run. "This is a nice shady spot. Probably the only *real* peaceful spot in the county." He was still huffing a little bit.

Hailey cast an admiring glance around. "It is great, isn't it. My dad made me and my sisters this swing when we were small." She motioned with her head to an old wooden flatbed trailer standing a few yards from the tree, its back wheels buried deep into the hard earth.

Jack didn't ask, but this had to be the flatbed Mr. Watson had tried to move.

Dee flashed Hailey a wide smile. "Higher!"

"Okay, higher." She gave Dee another giant shove.

Jack made a wide circle around the swing and stood beside the flatbed. "So this is where little girls come to play house and things like that, huh?"

"Heavens no, Jack! Play house? How nineteen fifty-two of you." She tossed him a look of mock shock before trying to tickle Dee's underarms as she swung past. "This is where little girls come to read and think and pretend that they're airplane pilots." She slowed the swing. "Good grief, we thought you knew that!"

Dee drug her feet across the ground and brought herself to a skidding stop. She hopped from the swing and ran to the flatbed, stepping from the tire to the top of the bed. She spun around with arms held straight, wing style. "Look, I'm an air-o-plane. See what I can do, Mr. Stins? I can be an air-o-plane." She hopped down and disappeared beneath the trailer.

Jack gasped and grabbed for her. He cast a worried look at Hailey. "Where's she going?"

Hailey touched a finger to her lips. "To our secret hiding place. Sometimes we read books together or work on letters and numbers. Sometimes we just talk. But no one can see us when we're under there. We are i-n-v-i-s-i-b-l-e," she spelled.

Jack wrinkled his brow. The thought of crawling underneath the flatbed made his chest tighten. A person could suffocate under there. It had to feel as if the whole world was falling down on top of you. A light film of perspiration reappeared on his face and he felt his knees weaken. "That's just not right. Make her come out of there," he urged.

Hailey didn't look up from the ants she was busy stomping with her work boot. "She's fine, Jack." Then she knelt and peered underneath the trailer. "Hey, Deedles, should we let Mr. Stinson come in to our secret hiding place? You could show him the A B C's we carved into the dirt."

He was just about to protest when a loud "No, thank you" came back at them.

Hailey shrugged at him. "You've been black balled from the secret hiding place."

"Too bad." A mock scowl touched his brow.

For the next twenty minutes, Jack and Hailey watched Dee crawl from beneath the trailer and swing awhile, then jump on the bed awhile. It surprised him that he was actually beginning to enjoy the squeals and child's non-stop chattering. He hadn't been around children much. Hadn't thought about them much, either. Who had time with the schedule he kept?

"Higher than the clouds, Mr. Stins! Come swing me high."

He walked across to give Dee a push on the swing. "Okay, but you can call me Jack."

The little girl grinned as she swung by him. "Jack! Jack! Swing me higher, Jack!"

Hailey tapped her watch. "Hate to break up the fun, you two, but us grownups have to get back to work."

Dee didn't complain. She skidded herself to a stop and jumped from the swing. "Race ya' Jack! Come on, Jack."

Hailey gave Jack an approving glance. "She likes your name."

He smiled back. "Obviously."

This time Hailey declined the invitation to run across the field. "You go ahead, Miss Busybody. I think we'll take a slow trip to the hangar and save some of our energy for work." She reached to pull the little girl to her and kiss the top of her damp curls. "Ask Granny Rinnie for apple juice. You're probably ready for a nap, too."

"Noooooooooo!" she protested in a fit of moans.

Hailey held up one finger. "One." Then added another. "Two."

Dee turned to run toward the house and Hailey called after her. "And ask her pretty please for some ice water out at the hangar."

"I will," she shouted over her shoulder, running with the energy only a six-year-old could muster after playing nonstop in the Texas heat.

Hailey wiped her brow. "Man, sometimes this heat is draining. Dallas is even hotter, though, isn't it? With all those buildings and concrete."

"A littler bit." He watched Dee zig-zag across the pasture on her way back to the house. "I wonder if we had that much energy when we were her age."

"Of course we did. If we could have only saved a bit for our old age." She dodged an ant hill. "Just think of the things we could accomplish in a day."

He was thoughtful. "I think you do pretty good for an old timer of…what? Twenty-two? Twenty-three?"

Her eyes twinkled. "Something like that. Actually, I'm twenty-six. And you?"

"Twenty-seven." His eyes focused on the ground as he walked. "Lately I've felt more like ninety-seven."

"I'll tell you. I've known a great many seventy and eighty-year-olds who had more going on than people less than half their age." She tapped a finger against her head. "It's all up here, you know. Age is nothing. Just a number."

"I'll remember that."

"See that you do, Mr. All-Kidding-Aside."

"If you call me that again I'll develop a complex."

She tossed her head, and walked backward, facing him with a teasing challenge. "Want to hear something that could give a person a complex?" When he nodded, she continued.

"Guess what my dad wanted to name me when I was born?"

He thought a moment. "I have no idea."

"Come on, guess!"

"Harvey."

She shook her head. "Try again."

"Airplane Jane." He chuckled at his own wit.

She stopped in her tracks. "Hey! That was good. You actually made a joke."

"I make jokes. When the occasion calls for it."

She started walking again. "I'm proud of you, Stinson. See, I told you there's hope."

"Okay, okay, don't gush over me. Now tell me what your father wanted to name you."

Her eyes were bright with merriment. "Cessna."

This time he was the one who halted abruptly. "Cessna?"

She nodded and continued walking. "Cessna. Can you believe it? Of course, that's before he bought his first Skycat. I could have been Cessna Holman. Or Skycat Holman." She shuddered. "Scary, isn't it?"

He threw his head back and let loose with an air-filling laugh. "Cessna? Now that's a good one. Cessna Comet Holman!"

He wiped at his eyes with the back of his hand. "I hope I didn't hurt your feelings. But Cessna? That's hilarious." His laughter turned into a warm smile. "What a cool sense of humor your father had."

"Didn't he though? Wouldn't you say I'm born to fly?" Her own smile held deep tenderness. "I have no choice. Dad always told me that I would soar across the sky. Thankfully, the one battle my mom *did* win was naming me."

"Hooray for your mom. I don't believe I could work for anyone named Cessna. They're our biggest competition."

The word "our" slipped from between his lips before he could remind himself that Cessna was no longer "his" competition. He was no longer a part of Brown Aeronautics. Changes were hard to get used to, but he would. In time. He smiled, hoping to recapture the light mood.

If she noticed his brief, solemn lapse, she didn't show it. She smiled back at him. "I like the Jack Stinson I'm seeing now. It's great to hear you laugh. Even if maybe I shouldn't be sharing such personal information about myself. Since you're just a short-timer and all." Her eyes glowed.

"I like it," he assured her. "And it's okay to share all this stuff. It'll make us stronger business associates." *If it works out that way.* He always liked getting to know his family business's employees and customers. It made him feel like he could be a better boss and offer better service. If only his dad could have understood that.

She agreed with him. "You're right. But I have a tendency to say whatever pops into my brain. While you seem more *refined*." She threw the word out with a good-natured grin.

"Refined? Of course I'm refined. Everybody looks refined to you compared to Neal and Paul."

"Hey! Those are my people."

"Oh, of course."

They walked in comfortable silence for a moment.

"But you, Jack—for all practical purposes, you're a stranger. I hardly know you." She turned herself back around and quickened the steps she took toward the hangar. "As much as I enjoy talking to you, who knows? You might take what you find out here and open a business nearby. You could be a spy. You could actually be in cahoots with the Watsons."

He glanced her way with a wide smile on his lips, trying to think of a clever comeback to her kidding. It took about two seconds for him to reconsider. "You couldn't possibly be serious. You think I could be a spy?"

"Never know." Her voice held a hint of mystery and she twisted her lips. "I mean, it's not impossible." She smiled at him and quickened her step.

He made no attempt to keep up with her faster pace. Instead, he let his eyes sweep their surroundings and followed a few steps behind. "Now I know you're kidding," he shouted at her back. "Cahoots with Neal and Paul."

He let loose with a huge smile. Even if she might actually be entertaining the ridiculous thought that he could be there with ulterior motives, he'd hate to see her succeed with anyone but him. He was pretty sure Hailey Holman would indeed succeed. And he already wanted it to be with him by her side.

He looked up and then all around him. *I'm already getting used to that airplane windsock fluttering on top of the hangar. And those cows grazing along the fence line. This could be paradise. With some changes.*

Maybe he could keep trying to talk to Rinnie. Maybe with time, she'd open up to him. And maybe with time, he'd let himself admit that he found Hailey Holman more than just a little bit fascinating.

He felt his ears burn. He could blame it on the sun beating down on him. Or heat stroke or lack of sleep making his mind wander. *Quit dreaming. Maybe I'd better stay focused on what's important. Like finding another job.*

CHAPTER EIGHT

Securing the latch on the hangar door, Hailey raised her eyes to the enormous cloudless sky. *Thank You, Lord. I'm trusting You.*

She believed Jack could very well be an answer to her dad's prayer, as well as to her own. Staring up into the heavens, she was oblivious to the approaching footsteps of her youngest sister.

"Are you lost in space somewhere?" Felicia stood close, her sweaty t-shirt still drenched from her efforts at cheerleading practice.

Hailey flinched. "You startled me, Diva. Didn't your mama teach you never to sneak up on people like that?" She offered her sister a good-natured swat on the backside.

"Are you kidding? My mom's the one who taught me to sneak up that way." She leaned against Hailey. "I love it because I get to hear the juiciest gossip that way."

Hailey waved her away. "Keep that gossip talk away from me and the same for that smell! I see you practiced outside in the heat again. I'll be glad when the air conditioning in the gym is fixed so you won't come home smelling like a gorilla anymore." She turned to hike toward the cottage. "Is Dee up from her nap? I promised to take her to feed the cows before we eat."

Felicia ignored her sister's question. "How's Mr. Wonderful Face?" She fluttered her lashes in Hailey's direction. "Anything exciting happening?"

"I'm sure I don't know who you're talking about." Hailey stared directly ahead as she walked. "Now be a big help and get Dee for me."

"Sure. Right. Like nobody's noticed how you look at him." Felicia swatted at a mosquito on her bare leg. "Like your heart doesn't beat out of your chest every time he's around." She crossed her hands across her own heart. "Whop, whop, whop."

"Stop it." Hailey stepped up onto the cottage porch. "You're making a real nuisance of yourself, little sister. I think it's *you* who thinks the new guy is Mr. Wonderful. To me, he's a coworker. Nothing more."

"Mr. Wonderful Face," Felicia corrected. "Funny how you keep saying he's just a '*coworker.*' And yeah, who wouldn't think he's adorable? But he's waaaaaay too old for me. He's more your style, older sister dear."

Hailey opened her mouth to defend herself, but Felicia interrupted with a snap of her fingers. "Oh, I almost forgot! Mom said, and I quote." Felicia put a scowl on her face. "I suppose that man can come to dinner. As long as he's here, we can't let him starve." The natural smile returned to her freckled face. "I think she's warming up to the idea, Sis. Maybe she'll ask him to stay herself. Maybe he'll fall madly in love with you, and—"

"I think you'd better land that space ship you're driving," Hailey interrupted. "Because you're definitely talking like you're suffering from air deprivation."

"Go ahead, throw those big words at me. I don't care. Just remember, you heard it here first. I'm the muse with the news. The snoop with the scoop. The lips with the tips. The—"

"The mouth that's gone south. Now get on to the house and deodorize yourself before we have to sit down at the table with clothespins on our noses. And tell Dee I'll be there to get her to feed the cows in five minutes." She swatted at her sister playfully.

Hailey stared at the door in front of her. Her heart *was* beating a bit faster. Her step *was* a bit livelier; she had to admit it to herself. But why is that so strange? It was because her mom was about to come around and the business was getting back on its feet. It's not because she was about to see *him*. Not at all.

She raised her hand and knocked on the cottage door. Her heart felt like it could hammer its way out of her chest. Irritation washed over her. If her youngest sister hadn't put the thoughts in her head, she wouldn't be feeling this…anxious.

Jack opened the door and leaned against the door frame. "Cessna, I didn't expect to see you again so soon."

His unexpected wit brought a surprised smile to her lips. "Why, Mr. Handsome Face—" Her eyes widened. Had she really said… no, no, no. Those words couldn't have slipped out of her mouth. She felt heat spread like wildfire into her cheeks.

He leaned his head back and a great peel of laughter escaped from his mouth.

She stood, feeling—for the first time that she could ever remember—utterly helpless.

"I…I…" Her mouth betrayed her. Her brain deserted her. She felt that she was standing in the middle of a swarm of laughing bees. "I…I…" She shook her head. "I suppose there's no way you're going to be gracious enough to pretend you didn't hear that."

He cupped his hand around his ear. "Excuse me? Did you say something? I guess I didn't hear you."

She struggled to regain her composure. There was no need to try to explain it was Felicia who called him Mr. Handsome Face, not her. Not that he wasn't attractive. She was honest with herself about his *attractiveness*. But she wasn't interested in Jack Stinson in that way.

She gave herself a mental jab. *He's a coworker. An employee.* Maybe he'd become a friend after they've been working together for a year. But she was not going to think of him as any more than that. She would shut that scary thought down before it crept from her mind to her heart and caused trouble.

Hailey mustered a simple smile. "My mom said you can come to dinner. Believe it or not, she actually said that. From what I hear, she practically begged for you to join us."

He observed her for a moment, the corners of his lips twitching. "Did she actually say she wants me there? Or that she'll tolerate me?"

"I think tolerated was more the sentiment. But then again, sometimes she only tolerates me, so don't feel like you're anything special."

He let out a deep chuckle.

Her face brightened, anxious to focus the attention back on him and away from her own silly thoughts. "Well, I can't believe it. Two laughs and a chuckle! In one day. Is this some sort of a record or something?"

"Come on now. I haven't really been *that* stuffy, have I, Miss Holman?" His face grew serious, but his eyes continued to hold the promise of a lighthearted smile.

"Well, I suppose you've never had to rely on your wit like I have. You've had your handsome face to open doors for you." *Make a joke, it throws 'em off every time.*

He stood relaxed, hands folded across his chest. "Oh, I don't know about that. I think you've done pretty fair in the looks department, yourself." He reached out to brush a strand of stray hair from her cheek.

She took a slight startled step back. *He can't beat me at my own game.* "I'm really hungry. I need to go feed the cows."

"You always feed the cows when you're hungry? Makes sense I guess."

"Dee promised the cows...I mean, I promised the Dee." She stomped her foot. "I'm trying to say that I promised Dee I'd take her to feed the cows."

He let loose with another genuine laugh. "Well, then you'd better keep your promise."

His smile grew half serious, half teasing. He didn't take his eyes off her face.

Hailey started to feel…itchy. If he'd only take his eyes away from hers for a split second, she'd make her getaway. But with her luck, she'd stumble down the stairs. She'd be tripped up by her own feet. Betrayed. Just as her tongue had double-crossed her a moment earlier when he first opened the door.

"Okay. All right." She scratched the back of her neck and attempted a composed front.

"Wash those greasy hands and we'll see you at the table. To eat. Thirty minutes." She backed away from the door. "Don't be late. You know my mom won't hold supper on you."

Hurrying to the house to fulfill her promise to Dee, she wondered how something this unthinkable could be happening to her.

She didn't have time for this right now. She was Web Holman's little Comet. And she'd fight that flirty, girly stuff trying to weasel its way into her heart to the bitter end.

• • •

Instead of plopping into bed as usual after her prayers, Hailey hesitated, peering into the mirror hanging over her sister's dresser. She picked up the pearl-handled hairbrush her dad had brought her from a business trip in France, and ran it through her dark hair.

She ran a finger across her chin, examining the skin she knew she too often took for granted.

Not that she didn't take care of her skin. It's just that she didn't make a fuss over it the way some women did. Certainly not the way her sisters and mom did, with all their creams and facials and wide-brimmed hats. Sunscreen and a baseball cap were about all Hailey usually needed.

She returned the brush to the dresser top and leaned closer to the reflection, scrutinizing her skin's texture, suddenly not satisfied with what she saw.

She'd never given the sprinkling of freckles across her nose much thought. Her mom had bought her a tube of concealer once and tried to give her a lesson on camouflaging her "imperfections." She'd laughed and her dad had shaken his head after Rinnie left the room. "Don't use that stuff, Comet. It'll smother your angel kisses."

The memory made her eyes grow misty. She swallowed hard. Her dad; her biggest fan.

Her mom, on the other hand…Hailey shook her head. Her mom made a lot of noise about Hailey's lack of interest in salon appointments and spa days.

She ran both hands through her hair. She liked her hair. It was wash and go. Long enough to push behind her ears and out of her way. Or make a pony tail. Who could climb around in the hangar in the Texas heat with hair flying everywhere?

She continued peering into the tell-all glass. "Maybe it is time for a few changes. Nothing drastic." She was fine with the way God made her, but maybe her mom and sisters were right. Maybe she could use a little *something*. She'd always liked her eyes because they were the color of the sky. But what would it be like to have eyes like…well, like Jack's? His eyes were like drops of chocolate. Chocolate Kisses.

She straightened her back and cocked her head at the reflection in the mirror. "Who are you staring at? What's the matter with you, anyway? A good-looking guy comes around and you start acting goofy all of a sudden."

"Who're you talking to in here?"

Hailey jumped. She turned to see her sleepy sister standing in the doorway.

"*Felicia!* What are you doing, trying to scare me half to death?" She put a hand over her thumping heart.

"What are *you* doing? You're scaring *me* half to death." Her younger sister leaned groggily on the doorframe. "You were looking in the *mirror.*"

Hailey cast her a look. "Ha. Ha. Very funny."

Felicia yawned and turned toward the hallway. "I'm going back to bed. I must be having some really weird psycho dream."

"Wait."

She turned back around to face Hailey, her eyes blinking slowly. "Hailey, come on, what? I need to get some sleep."

"I could use a little help here."

"*A little*?" Even half asleep Felicia could dish it out as good as Hailey.

Hailey waved her off. "You know, never mind. Go back to bed."

Felicia didn't argue. "Goodnight."

Hailey turned her back on the mirror and climbed into bed, reaching for the light on the bedside table. She chuckled at herself. Big ol' hair and mud packs and eye liner. That was for divas.

Her eyes closed and her mind went to work. Someday she supposed she'd have to redeem the gift certificate her mom had given her Christmas before last. Or was that the Christmas before the Christmas before last?

A frown crept across her lips. Whenever it was, giving Web Holman's oldest daughter a certificate for "The Works" at Beth's Salon & More was pointless.

Hailey turned to the other side and then rolled again to settle on her back, staring up at the ceiling with her hands tucked behind her head. She finally let out an irritated sigh. She obviously wasn't getting to sleep any time soon.

"Lord," she whispered into the darkness. "I'm feeling something I've never felt before. I'm feeling like a..." She stopped herself. "I'm feeling like a woman, I guess. I mean, for heaven's sake, I'm twenty-six and never really thought much about this before. Not seriously anyway. It's natural, I know, and someday I want to find that special guy, but it's *complicated* right now."

She let her eyes slip shut. "Okay, Lord, complicated is nothing for you, I know that. But there's some sort of…attraction I feel for this guy. And I don't like it. Even if he did seem pretty boring at first, which, you and I both know is a total turn-off. Anyway, today I saw something special in him."

She blinked into the stillness of the room and reflected on the past six months. *It seems that I'm the only one here who remembers who Dad really was. I don't want to hide him away with his box of baseball caps and his shaving stuff. I don't want to let go of his dream.*

She swallowed the lump that lodged in her throat. "I have to be the one who lives for him, now. I am Web Holman's daughter, and I thank You for the chance to continue his dream. Nothing can stand in the way of me doing his will…and Yours. I know everybody gets sick of hearing me say it, but I get so *weary* of being told I can't do this." She let her eyelids close on the tears that threatened to spill from her eyes. "Amen."

The next thing Hailey knew, her eyes were open again and she was tiptoeing to Felicia's room. She closed the door behind her. She couldn't afford to wake her mom.

Making her way across the room, she bent over her sister's bed, tapping Felicia's shoulder gently.

"Huh? What's wrong?" Her sister bolted upright and grabbed at Hailey's arm.

"Nothing," she whispered her assurance. "I have to ask you something."

Felicia stared through the dark, obviously trying to focus on the shadow of her oldest sister's face. "You woke me up to ask me something? I find you staring at yourself in the mirror earlier. There's definitely something wrong."

Hailey lowered herself softly to sit on the side of the bed. She leaned closer to her sister but hesitated with the words she wanted to say.

"Tell me before you drive me crazy."

"You can't even tell Mom. Or Lindsey."

Felicia let out an exasperated sigh. "I promise. Now just tell me!"

Hailey took in a big gulp of air. "You know that silly little makeover you're always wanting to do on me?"

"Grrrrrr." Felicia plopped back on her pillow with a groan. "You woke me up to tell me never ever to mention that dumb makeover to you again?"

Hailey reached for Felicia's shoulders and tried to pull her back up to face her. "No," she whispered. "*Listen*. Let's do it."

The silence between them hung like a thick black curtain in the dark room. It seemed to take a few moments for the impact of Hailey's words to sink in, but when they finally did, Felicia shot up and did a little bounce on her bed, squealing.

Hailey clapped a hand over her sister's mouth. "Shhhhhh!" She suddenly felt silly. "Listen, kiddo. Never mind. Bad idea. Forget you saw me. In fact, you didn't see me. This was all a dream." She stood, continuing to hold her hand over Felicia's mouth, and pushing her sister back gently until her dark pony tail touched the pillow. "Now lay down. Close your eyes. And don't say one word."

She removed her hand and started away from Felicia's bed.

Before she reached the door, a quiet voice whispered into the darkness. "We really wouldn't have to do much to your hair. Maybe just some barrettes or something. But you definitely need some plum eye shadow in the creases of your eyelids. That would really bring out your gorgeous blue eyes."

Hailey turned back, once again settling on the edge of the bed next to her sister. "You think?"

"Sure." Felicia stretched and stuffed the extra pillow beside her behind her head. "We could fix you up like when you went to the prom with Bradley. On second thought, let's fix you up better! Hey, I saw Bradley in town at the bank a few weeks ago."

Hailey was pleased. "Bradley's a good guy. He was always a good friend. Were Kaitlin and the kids with him?"

"Yep, their kids are so cute. Why didn't you and Bradley ever, you know, *like* like each other?"

She shrugged. "We were just buds. There wasn't anything else there." He wasn't *the one*.

"I'd like to have a boyfriend."

"Felicia," Hailey shook her head. "Don't just have a boyfriend because you think it's the cool thing to do."

"I might wait until I go to college. All the guys here are like brothers or cousins. We grew up together."

Hailey understood. "Don't rush it or force it. That's been my motto."

"Exactly," Felicia let out an exasperated breath. "You're in a slump. Have you even been out with a guy since high school? No. You've been buried in airplanes and flying and books and everything *but* finding time for a relationship. Now you're talking about a guy you just met like he's something special. It's so out of the blue. It's weird."

Hailey let out a deep sigh and stood up, making her way back to the door. She reached for the doorknob and without turning around, whispered back to her sister. "Do you want to do this or not?"

"Are you kidding? I'm all over it!"

"Okay, well. Quick. Before I come to my senses."

"Tomorrow after lunch? As soon as Mom leaves for her Garden Club meeting."

"Okay, okay. Don't make some big deal about this."

"I won't. Good night, Hailey."

Hailey could hear the smile in her little sister's voice. "Good night, Diva."

She tread softly back to her room, muttering to herself. "Why in the world now, of all times, did a guy like Jack Stinson have to show up?" Reality snapped her brain. "Oh yeah. I invited him."

CHAPTER NINE

Hailey checked her watch for the tenth time. One seventeen. Just three minutes later than the last time she checked it.

She dug another chocolate kiss from her pocket, unwrapped it, and popped it into her mouth. Any minute now.

The sound of Felicia's tennis shoes slapping against the concrete made her heart leap. She sucked in a deep breath.

Fleeting fragments of peace eluded Hailey's grasp and she felt her insides consumed by a strange sensation. Could this be…No. It couldn't be what other people experienced as *panic*. That feeling wasn't allowed in her range of emotions.

The makeover hadn't even begun, and it was already provoking a drastic personality change.

Felicia motioned to her sister. "Hi, Hailey. Hi, Jack," she called louder than usual.

Jack waved his hello from the cockpit and continued working.

Hailey made her way casually from the door to stand beside the aircraft. "Hey, Jack. I have some things to take care of. So I won't be around for a couple of hours."

He looked away from the odometer he was working on and grinned down at her from the cockpit. "Alright."

She stood looking up at him, fully conscious of the ticking clock that decreed her immediate departure. Digging for another chocolate kiss, she came up with a handful of empty wrappers instead.

Great. Just when she needed it most.

"Uh, listen, Jack. I was thinking maybe I'd take you to see some of beautiful Barnes this evening. How about an early supper at my favorite place? My treat."

He smiled down at her from the cockpit. "Sounds good. But I'm buying. Your family's fed me enough." He stripped a wire from beneath the dash before glancing back her way. "I guess we're going to your uncle's diner since it's the only place around?" He seemed genuinely pleased. "In fact, you ladies ask your mom to join us. Maybe we can all get to know each other a little better."

Hailey opened her mouth, but before she could respond, Felicia hurried to decline gracefully. "That sounds great, Jack, but I have to practice for my piano recital and Mom…Mom's on a diet."

"Your mom's on a diet?" He tossed them both a quizzical look. "What for? She couldn't weigh a hundred and ten pounds."

Felicia shook her head. "Women. Will we ever understand 'em?"

Jack gave a decisive shake of his head before turning his attention back to Hailey.

"Well, I guess it's just the two of us then. Unless you want to back out on me."

Her flustered voice threatened to betray her. She laughed to hide her agitation. "I asked you, didn't I, you big lug." She propped her hands on her hips, wondering how in the world she'd finished off two pockets full of candy since lunch without realizing it.

"Be ready at five," she issued the order with more control than she felt.

"It's a date, then."

She adjusted her smile. "I wouldn't call it a date, actually. I'd call it more of an appointment. Or an outing, maybe." she said, wiping her perspiring palms along the front of her jeans. "It's just food."

She bit her lip and turned toward Felicia, who stood waiting at the hangar door.

I'm supposed to be the confident, funny one. Felicia is the primpy, flirty one. Lindsey, the other diva, is the sophisticated, polished one. And Jack's the serious, dignified one. And for some ridiculous, outrageous reason, I want to impress him so badly.

She fought the urge to scream "Never mind" at him. *As soon as this makeover foolishness is done I'll regain my rightful place as family jokester before permanent damage can be done to my reputation. Oh, Lord. What am I doing?*

As Felicia linked her arm through her sister's, and the two started toward the house, Hailey felt like a lamb being led to the slaughter.

What in the world had she gotten herself into now?

•••

Jack took one look at the vaguely familiar figure swaying gently on the porch swing. He felt his mouth drop open but seemed powerless to push the words out.

"Hailey? Is that you?" Dumb question. Of course it was her. He'd know those eyes anywhere.

"Who else would you expect to be sitting here waiting on a slowpoke like you?" She stopped the swing with a dainty sandaled, perfectly pedicured foot and stood as he approached.

Was this angel in white the same woman who departed from the hangar a few hours before? The same woman with grease stains on her work shirt and rust flakes in her hair? He recovered his thoughts slowly. "You look absolutely..." he searched for a word to exchange for stunning, beautiful or gorgeous. "Wow."

She gave her ruffled white skirt a twirl. "Oh, this old thing?" The amusement flickering in her sapphire eyes was accompanied by a hint of uncharacteristic apprehension.

She met him at the steps and he reached a hand forward to assist. "Why, thank you, Mr. Stinson." She laid a soft, perfectly nail-polished hand in his and stepped from the porch.

"You're welcome, Miss Holman." He released her hand reluctantly and fought the urge to tell her that she looked like an absolute angel. Minus the wings. Actually with wings, he thought with a smile. But no airplane talk. Not tonight.

His brain warned him that she may bolt and run if he overwhelmed her with flattery. *It's probably best to keep some of my thoughts to myself.*

Jack stole another look at her. *Don't tell her she's glowing. And don't stare at her lips.*

Don't tell her she's prettier than any model or movie star you've ever seen.

"I'm hungry," he said. "And looking forward to seeing the big city of Barnes. And by the way, you look great."

She tossed her head in an exaggerated effort, swinging the hair around her shoulders. "Oh, this is just how us Barnes girls always look." She offered him an admiring glance. "You don't look so bad yourself."

"Well, thanks. I try." He really wanted to tell her how much he liked the way her face seemed delicate and strong at the same time. How much he's already become accustomed to her boldly refreshing, natural beauty and how fun she was, even when she was driving everybody crazy with her one-track mind. *Especially* then.

"So, I take it I'm not under dressed for this favorite place of yours."

She eyed his navy slacks and navy and white striped button down. "Where we're going, you can wear anything you like. There's no dress code."

He held the gate open for her. "That's good. What does your uncle serve at his diner beside chicken fried steak?"

"A variety." She swished her skirt as she passed through.

He closed the gate behind them. "In other words, you're not telling me anything more until we get there."

She pointed a glossy mauve polished fingernail at him. "Bingo."

• • •

Pulling her Dodge pickup onto the road, Hailey fought the sudden urge to pull the barrettes from her hair and grab a tissue to rescue her lashes from the three coats of mascara Felicia had layered around her eyes. She ran her tongue along Plum Passion lips and grimaced. Yuk, she sputtered inwardly, feeling her resolve to tolerate this made-up business slip away. *This stuff tastes like flavored wax.* "I want my Dr. Pepper flavored lip gloss."

Jack eyed her in disbelief. "They make a Dr. Pepper flavored lip gloss?"

I said that out loud? "The bluebonnets are blooming like crazy." She mentally patted herself on the back. Nice recovery.

"They sure are. Beautiful. They make a Dr. Pepper flavored lip gloss?"

"Sure do. Know what I like about wildflowers? They're just themselves. They're genuine." Hailey felt an uncomfortable tug at her heart. She'd always insisted on being herself at all costs, whether it pleased others or not. And now here she was, driving her pickup down the same dirt road she learned to drive on as a gangly tomboy teenager, and she was too uncomfortable to enjoy it.

She missed her blue jeans.

I'm not cut out for this made-up stuff. She plucked a tissue from inside the console and rubbed at her lips. Then fished in the cup holder for her stash of lip gloss and hair bands. She swiped a layer across each lip. "Man, that's better!"

She glanced his way. Jack only smiled. He seemed to be enjoying the view as much as she was. "Don't you love the way the wildflowers are just randomly scattered around like they fell out of heaven? My mom works so hard on her roses, and they're gorgeous, but this is amazing," she said.

"Well, I guess there's no such thing as an ugly flower. But I think you might be right. About the wildflowers falling out of heaven."

A pensive reflection touched her. "You know what? My dad and I, we're wildflowers. My mom and my sisters, they're roses."

"That's interesting. I never thought of that." He studied her face. "And what am I?"

She didn't hesitate. "You're a begonia. Strong. Solid. Stunning."

He drew his lips in. "I like that."

"Well, you should." She tapped her brake. "It's a compliment."

Reaching their first turn off, and without fanfare, Hailey tugged on the barrettes and shook the hairspray from her hair. Then she reached down and pulled the sandals from her feet and chucked them behind the seat, issuing him a satisfied grin. "So tell me, in your manly opinion. Most men prefer roses, don't they? To wildflowers?"

He watched her with interest. "Wildflowers are great. So are roses." He shrugged. "They're both great."

"Sure." She slowed the pickup and turned onto a narrow dirt road. "But if a guy has a choice between a rose and a wildflower, which would he choose?"

"Depends on the guy."

She wanted to tell him how dense guys could be. *Which would you choose, Jack Stinson?* "I've seen the way men look at roses."

"And what kind of look is that?" There was no challenge in his voice. He was genuinely interested in her answer.

She widened her eyes and held her mouth open in a mock gaping gawk, swiping her hand at imaginary drool on her chin.

"We don't."

"You do! A lot of men do, anyway."

He shifted in his seat to turn toward her, resting his arm across the back of her seat. "Maybe so, the heathens."

She let out a laugh.

"Well, not trying to change the subject or anything, but begonias are my mom's favorite flower."

She slipped a bare foot on the brake again and made another turn. "I like being a wildflower. They're just themselves. Know what I mean?"

"I do. But I also think that roses are themselves as well."

"Ah, true, Jack. But wildflowers can thrive with just the basics. Water, dirt, sunshine. That's the kind of life I want to live. Basic. Roses need pruning and special care." Her shoulders rose and fell quickly. "That's just the way God made them."

He seemed to ponder her statement as he shifted his head forward to survey the upcoming scenery. "That's fine for you. But do you think other people are wrong for seeing things differently than you?" He faced her again. "For instance, say you want to be this way. Basic. And someone close to you doesn't. They were created to be a rose or a tulip. Or a daisy. If you have to live together, how do you get along without infringing on the other's right to be themselves?"

She twisted her lips in thought. "Well, I suppose." The realization of whom he was speaking of hit her. "You're sharp, Stinson. But my situation isn't nearly as simple as you're trying to make this whole flower scenario sound."

"I never said it was simple. I was only wondering what solution you'd offer to someone in a similar predicament, that's all."

"Sure, sure. But you never really told me, Jack. Are you a wildflower man or a roses man?" *When in doubt, change the subject.*

She certainly wasn't planning to spend an evening listening to him tell her how wrong she was about reopening the business without her mom's consent. She could have stayed home and been beat over the head with that message.

He pondered with narrowed eyes and lips drawn thoughtfully. "That's the big question. You want to know which I'd prefer?"

"Yeah, what type of women did you date in Cryder, Texas? Or woman." It suddenly occurred to her that there could be someone significant in his life. Maybe someone he was trying to get over. Her heart took a little dive toward her stomach.

He let out a resolved chuckle. "Date? My dear, I had no time for dates. I barely had time for a haircut every few weeks."

"That's too bad."

"Yeah, I can tell you're all choked up about it." His brown eyes met her profile with obvious approval.

She tossed him a sideways glance. "I am. Truly. Choked." She conjured up a cough.

"So what about you? What type of men do you date in Barnes, Texas? Begonias? Gerber daisies?"

"Date? Are you serious? I barely have time for a haircut every few *months*."

An expression of satisfaction danced around his face. "What a shame."

"Indeed!" She laughed at his obvious pleasure. "I hear you choking, too."

They drove in comfortable silence for a moment. Jack cast another look her way. "You really do look great. But, to be truthful, I think I like the denim Hailey better. So there, I said it. Don't be offended."

"Well, so do I, so there, and the truth doesn't offend me," she tossed back at him before a full force laugh left her lips. "I don't think I dressed up this much for any of those senior year special events we're supposed to attend. So I suppose now you're going to think you're something really special."

"I don't think I'm something special, and I don't care if you wear a potato sack and twigs in your hair." His eyes blazed playfully in her direction. "And who did you go to those fancy senior year functions with? I thought you never had time for dates."

"Oh, you know how it was. High school. Everybody goes to the prom. I went with a buddy of mine. Bradley. We were best buds more than anything. Hung out together, sang in the church choir, promised we'd marry each other someday if we couldn't find anyone else to put up with us."

"What happened to ol' Bradley?"

She flashed a wide grin. "He found someone to put up with him."

Before he could ask, she offered her explanation. "Bradley was always a super nice guy, but when he went off to college he changed." She glanced over at him with her best smug "of course" look. "He wanted a rose. He wouldn't settle for a wildflower anymore."

"His loss."

She shrugged. "Maybe. Oh, and I took another friend, Mark Merket, to the Athletic Banquet."

"What happened to him? Don't tell me he married a rose, too."

She wasn't sure if he'd laugh or want to run now. "Ugh, well, after our date he announced he wanted to go into the priesthood." She paused and pushed a stray hair behind her ear. "Some say I had something to do with that. But I don't think so."

He let out a loud laugh and reached across to pat her shoulder anyway. "You poor thing. That's gotta hurt. But I don't know that I'd take that too personally. Those two guys just had different *callings*. Right?"

"Obviously!" She let loose with a laugh of her own and swung her truck onto a long dusty driveway. She was beginning to allow herself to feel decidedly comfortable with him. And it felt good.

"Bradley got to be so ambitious once he left Barnes. Not ambitious in a good way.

Ambitious like step-on-people-to-get-where-I-want-to-go ambitious. That was my opinion, anyway." She went on. "Can you picture me as a big city lawyer's wife?"

"Sure, if that's what you wanted."

She braked in front of a huge red barn and turned the ignition key to off.

She swiveled her head to face him. "Sorry, that was a judgmental statement, but you know how I feel. We all just need to be who we are. Whether it's a lawyer, a pilot…" She shrugged. "Or a man of the cloth."

He agreed with a knowing nod. "I've never disagreed with you on that point." He looked as if he wanted to say more, but she hurried to open the truck door and step out into the breezy west Texas air.

Taking the sides of the skirt she'd borrowed from her sister Lindsey's closet in each of her hands, Hailey waved the cloth around her in the breeze. "Look at this. We could dress two families with this one piece of material."

He bit his lip to stifle a grin. "Maybe three."

"What was I thinking?" She wiggled her toes in the thick dust and squinted against the rapidly sinking sun. "Let's go inside and watch the sunset."

"Go inside? This is a barn."

"Of course it's a barn. Where did you think my favorite place to eat would be?" She flung him a deliberately incredulous look. "You actually thought we were going to some stuffy old restaurant?" She headed for the back end of her pickup and he followed.

"No, actually I thought we were going to your uncle's place."

Opening the tailgate she reached for one of the baskets sitting in the truck bed. "Jack, you are so funny." She pointed to the farthest basket from his reach. "That's the heavy one."

He reached in and retrieved the lighter one first and handed it to her, then he grabbed onto the heaviest one for himself. "What's so funny about me thinking we were going to your uncle's place?"

"We are. Wanna hand me that quilt?"

"You are so totally confusing me right now." He draped the colorfully patched quilt on top of the basket in his hand.

She wrapped both hands around the wicker handle of the basket she carried. "Ready?"

He nodded and circled his arms around his cumbersome load. "Your uncle has the only diner in town. We're going to your uncle's place. But we're here? With food?"

"This is my uncle's farm. My favorite place to eat. The diner's great, but this place..." She stepped around a patch of brown grass. "Yikes, stickers."

Jack followed close behind as she led him around to the side of the barn. "This belongs to your uncle with the diner or is this another uncle?"

"Uncle Frank. The one who owns the diner. My only living uncle. Great, huh? I'm afraid they'll sell it one day, but for now..." Happiness covered her face. "It's all ours!"

His eyes roamed their surroundings. "I like it."

She knew her smile radiated her pleasure. "Just wait. You haven't seen anything yet. Remember, I told you I was going to show you more of Barnes. You're in for a real treat." She led him forward a few steps further until they reached a faded red wooden door. She halted and set her basket on the ground.

Jiggling the doorknob, she cast a confident look over her shoulder at him. "There's a trick to this," she said, leaning her right shoulder against the door, twisting and lifting the knob with her left hand, and pushing up on the door as she pushed it open against her weight. The door flew open with a bang against the barn wall.

Jack shifted his load in his arms. "Nice move."

"Thanks, it's all in the wrist. And the shoulder." She reached for her basket. "I come here all the time,"

"That's too bad. I was hoping since you're such a wallflower…I mean, wildflower, that I'm the only man you've ever brought out here. Bradley and Father Mark ever get to see this favorite place of yours?" His brown eyes teased her mercilessly.

She stepped away from him and into the shadowy barn. "Nope, as a matter of fact, you are the only male to darken this door. But don't let that go to your head."

CHAPTER TEN

As intrigued as he was with Miss Hailey Holman, Jack had no intention of letting this excursion go to his head. The open doorway cast just enough light for him to detect the image of a steep set of stairs several feet into the barn. "Is there a light switch around here anywhere?"

"What do you need a light switch for?" She propped the wooden door open with a brick resting just inside the door.

"In case you haven't noticed, it's dark in here."

She disappeared beyond some thin streams of light filtering through the barn and shortly after, the distinctive sound of match striking against wood met his ears. A gentle flickering glow filled the barn and she reappeared, brandishing a kerosene lamp. "Is this enough light for you, Mr. City Boy?" Her voice held good-natured teasing.

"It's enough if we're able to see where we're going." He walked back into the daylight to retrieve the picnic basket she'd deposited in front of the door. "Even city boys like to see where they're walking. Hate to run into an unwelcome surprise."

"I understand. We are in a barn, after all." She transferred the lamp to one hand and gathered a handful of skirt in the other. "Thanks for getting that other basket. Come on, you're gonna love this place."

They made their way across and she started up the steps, stopping to stomp the dusty earth from her bare feet. "And to think the pioneer women wore eighty pounds of clothes every day. This get-up is heavy."

He chuckled as he halted a step below her. "If they could do it, I have absolutely no doubt that you can, as well." They proceeded up the stairs. "So you say they serve good food here, huh?"

"The best." She didn't look back, but continued making her way up the steps. "When we were growing up, my sisters and I, and our cousins, spent a lot of Sunday afternoons out here. We'd play up here for hours while the grownups played dominoes out under the trees and Uncle Frank barbecued. Pretty much every Sunday after church." She reached the top step. "I can almost taste that sweet mesquite sauce now."

His mouth started to water. "That does sound good. I don't suppose you have any of that barbecue in one of these baskets." As heavy as his basket was, he figured she must have a little bit of everything in it. It wouldn't totally surprise him to find all of those sisters and cousins she'd mentioned, waiting beyond the top of these steps to join them. He'd already learned that nothing— absolutely nothing could surprise him where she's concerned. He climbed the last step and anticipated her next move.

She dropped the folds of material from her full skirt and strode ahead to stand before two enormous windows covered by thick wooded shutters. She extinguished the lamp and set it on the window frame. "I don't think you'll be too disappointed about missing Uncle Frank's barbecue this evening." She clasped her hands in front of her like a small child readying herself to unwrap a Christmas present. "I promised to show you more of Barnes. Ready?"

He relieved his arms of the weighty baskets and quilt and headed toward her, watching as she flipped the latches on the shutters and pushed them open with a burst of delight.

A sudden explosion of light filled the dimly lit loft and his eyes beheld a healthy view of the Barnes countryside. He opened his mouth to speak, but the words didn't come right away. "This is incredible," he finally managed in an awestruck whisper.

She stood beside him, hands clasped beneath her chin. "Welcome to the loft. My other secret hiding place."

He was struck by the beauty stretching before them, and beside him. A tranquil awareness washed through him. "This is amazing. Miles and miles of just…wow. Those oak trees are huge. The pastures go on forever. It's all so green."

He couldn't say anything else. All he could do was let his eyes drink in the scene. The wide open pastures, the grazing livestock dotted along the roving land. He nodded his head toward one of the fields. "Are there any fish in that pond?"

She craned her neck. "In Mr. Jackson's pond? Best catfish Uncle Frank's ever fried up in his diner."

"Look how the sun reflects off the water, it's almost too brilliant to look at. Like millions of diamonds flashing at the same time. And the sky…the bluest I can ever remember."

She gazed through the big double windows with him. "Didn't I tell you you'd love this? I come here when I want peace and quiet. I can hear God better."

He wanted to ask what she meant, but he didn't want to risk giving her a segway into a theological sermon right now. "I thought you thrived on the roar of planes and stirring up a fuss with your mom."

She smiled. "I obviously do, right?" Her eyes were on him for a moment before turning her attention back to the Barnes countryside.

"Do you ever do any fishing down at Mr. Jackson's pond?" he asked.

"Some."

He willed himself to keep his gaze straight ahead on the scenery beyond the massive windows.

"I can take you there sometime, if you'd like." She looked away from the view long enough to push a strand of hair from her eyes.

He gave her a brief nod. "I haven't been fishing since…I don't know, since before I started shaving. I doubt I'd know how to bait a hook anymore." He hadn't done anything just for fun in so long, he doubted he truly knew how to do much of anything along those lines right now. Not that he wouldn't welcome the challenge of relearning.

She tossed her head and laughed. "It's sort of the same as roller skating, I suppose. You never really forget how, you just get sort of rusty at it." She gave him a lighthearted pat on the back. "Don't worry. I could always bait your hook for you."

"No, thanks. I'd never hear the end of that one."

A contented smile settled across her face.

The two stood side by side, watching the fiery sun leisurely vanish to the other side of the earth. Both seemed enraptured by the scarlet glow lingering in the sky, and by the display casting a tranquil hue over the countryside.

Jack finally broke the silence. "Tell me more about your dad," he asked quietly. He found himself intrigued by the man this daughter loved so completely. The man who, in this daughter's eyes, was as near to perfect as a human got. The man who obviously influenced her and left such an indelible print on her heart. Perhaps a print in the shape of a comet racing across the sky.

She didn't hurry her answer, but seemed to linger, still captivated by the view. When she answered his question, her voice was filled with tenderness.

"This is one of those places where I feel closest to God. And to my dad. I can almost see him soaring in the Skycat. Like a silver and red decoration in the sky." She offered him a soft smile. "What do you want to know about Web Holman that you haven't seen of him around our home?"

"I guess what it is that makes you want to be so much like him."

She didn't hesitate. "That's pretty easy to answer. I've always wanted to be like him. Always. He was just so full of life. And God's goodness and love and…everything. Everything that anyone would ever want to be or want the person they love to be."

"Your mom has a lot of that life in her. Don't you think?"

She drew her lips in. "Somewhat. Sometimes. Ok yes, of course she does. Don't get me wrong, my mom's precious. Other than her obvious one big *flaw*," she half kiddingly exaggerated the word.

"Flaws." He kept his eyes on the fading horizon. "We all have 'em."

"To one degree or another, we sure do." She smiled at his profile before returning her own gaze to the scene before them. "I know I do."

Her posture relaxed and she attempted to tuck her hands into pockets that weren't there. She tossed him an "I miss my blue jeans again" look and continued, clasping her hands behind her back instead, and returning her gaze to the now graying sky.

"Dad even knew how to make everyday chores a celebration. He was always good-natured, always joking about things other people got high blood pressure over. His whole life, everything he did seemed sanctioned somehow. As if God Himself ordained this man to be the rock of this little piece of earth." She turned her eyes to him. "He loved everybody whether they loved him or not. He sure didn't wait for anyone to deserve to be loved before he loved them. I wish you could have met him, you'd know what I mean."

It stung a little. His own dad required proof of worthiness in triplicate and notarized before anyone passed the Marshall Stinson test. And then you were never sure whether his good graces were going to last a minute, an hour, or a day and a half.

Jack felt as if he almost did know Web Holman. That was, if Hailey's view of him was accurate. If she wasn't just making a hero out of him, forgetting the imperfections as humans do after a death "So you've patterned your life after your father's."

"And fallen about two hundred miles short. Few people were like my dad, Jack. He believed in asking himself what Jesus would do in every situation. That's why I believe with all my heart that I *must* continue his dream. If it was the right thing for him, then I know without a speck of doubt that someone must continue on."

The comment slapped at Jack's heart. *I wish I could say that about my own father.* "That's admirable. Who wouldn't want to believe they were doing something that someone else saw as so valuable they'd want to follow in your footsteps?"

He thought back to how it was when his great-granddaddy died several years ago. His passing left only his granddad to try to keep Marshall in line. When granddad passed away nine months ago, that left the brunt of it on Jack. The last person Marshall would ever listen to.

For as long as he could remember, his mom had done her best to make Marshall see that he was alienating his own family as well as anyone associated with Brown Aeronautics. She was always the glue holding it all together. Nurturing and openly praying for them all. The word vibrated in his ears and his thoughts stood still. Praying. For the entire family. And now with him away from home, she must be praying even harder.

He searched Hailey's face. "I can't fully grasp what you're telling me. What about your mom? Your parents' dreams seemed as completely opposite as anything I can imagine. You're saying one was one hundred percent right and the other, one hundred percent wrong?"

Even as he heard himself say it, he knew that was the case in his home. The warmth of his mother; the coolness of his father. The goodness of his mother; the hardness of his father. Still, there had to be something good that he'd forgotten, something that made his mother fall in love with his father in the first place. And something that kept her with him.

"The only absolute I know," Hailey stated with conviction "is God's love. No matter how much my mom fumed or feared, Dad's joy was flying. He still took me flying. He still allowed me to have flying lessons. He still encouraged me in the business. If I didn't believe with all my heart that my mom's fears were unreasonable, I'd question myself just like you're questioning me now. She's always been this way."

Her shrug was resigned. "More so now, since Dad's been gone, but I suppose that's part of her grieving for him."

Jack still had his doubts. "Even the short while I've been around your mom, I don't think she's the type of person who particularly *enjoys* conflict. Especially between the two of you."

"Of course she's not. But when it comes to flying, she loses all reason. She kinda' goes overboard. The past is the past and we grow from it. Know what I mean?" Without waiting for his answer, she turned from the window and reached for the quilt draped over one of the picnic baskets. "I'm starved. Let's eat."

He stood a moment longer, not ready for the conversation to end. "Don't you think you should have more of an open mind toward your mother?"

"My mind is open, hers isn't." She held the quilt in her arms, ready to spread it over the straw covered floor. "Now, are you going to help me, or are you going to stand there beating a dead horse?"

He hesitated for a moment before reaching for the baskets and holding them up while she lowered the colorful covering to the floor. He set the baskets to rest on the quilt and waited for her next move.

It was obvious she was tired of discussing her mom's reservations, but somehow, before the evening ended, he was going to interject some thoughts on compromise into her one-track mind.

Hailey reached for the kerosene lamp on the window ledge and set it between the two baskets, easing herself down onto the quilt and arranging the acres of skirt out of her way. She opened the basket closest to her and peered inside. "I hope you're as hungry as I am because we have a mountain of food here."

"I know. I'm the one who hauled that one up those stairs."

"Oh, don't worry, you'll be glad you did." Her mouth curved into a radiant smile. "This is the basket with the cold stuff." She reached in and named each item as she extracted it from the basket and set it before them. "Cantaloupe. Strawberries. Grapes. Tossed salad."

She removed a Thermos and handed it to him, then continued with the parade of food. "Iced tea. Sliced limes. Butter. And of course," she pulled out a small white bottle, "my famous buttermilk ranch poppy seed dressing."

"Sounds amazing."

Pushing the first basket aside, she moved the second one closer and peered in. "And here are," she reached inside. "The rolls, which I remember you said were your weakness." She smiled. "And jalapeño pie." She waved the plate of pie under his nose, obvious pleasure covering her face.

He smiled at her childlike enthusiasm and wondered if Web Holman had been aware of how much his daughter actually did take after him. She seemed a perfect replica of the things he'd heard about Web. Smart, lively, talented, caring—stubborn.

Hailey had a way of making the name "Dad" synonymous with words like honor, adoration and love. Jack knew deep in his heart that he loved his own dad. Hopefully, time and distance would dull some of the anger he felt. But he had to wonder: Was it really anger? Or just disappointment? His father simply hadn't been someone who Jack felt he could pattern his life after. Or sadly, even look up to.

He watched intently as Hailey emptied the rest of the basket onto the quilt, arranging a setting for each of them. Finally, she placed two heavy wooden candlesticks between the settings and handed him a box of kitchen matches. "Would you do the honors?"

He took the matches from her hand. "This really is an impressive spread," he said, striking a match and touching the flame to the white wick of each candle. He waved the match out. "You certainly thought of everything."

"Don't sound so surprised." She took the cooled match from his hand and dropped it into the basket. "I do love to cook, that's the one thing I got from Rinnie that my sisters didn't."

He pointed to the pie. "That looks good. What exactly is it?"

"You've never had jalapeño pie? Oh, that's right, I forget. That's country folk food." She unwrapped the pie. "Just jalapeños, eggs and cheese baked together. Help yourself."

She poured a goblet full of iced tea and handed it to him before uncovering each container of food. "That's as much as you're going to be waited on." She settled back in front of her own plate. "Want to bless the food, or should I?"

"Go for it." That was something he never planned to do. Pray out loud.

She immediately bowed her head. "Lord, thank You so much for all You provide for us. Bless this food and bless the time we get to spend relaxing and enjoying the beautiful world You made. We love You so much. In Jesus' name we pray, amen."

He surveyed the feast before him, watching her cut into the pie. The one with all the cheese. "Except for that," he pointed to the pie. "This is pretty healthy stuff. I'm surprised we're not having Hershey Kisses and chocolate pie with chocolate chip cheesecake and chocolate milk on the side."

She munched on a grape. "You laugh, but actually, that very menu did cross my mind." She plucked another grape from the stem. "Seriously, I eat my share of sweets, I guess that's my comfort food. But I'm really pretty health conscious."

He wanted to tell her that she looked pretty healthy to him, but thought better of it. For this first time alone with her, he reminded himself, he'd better stick to a safe subject. She sipped on her iced tea. "Okay, you've heard the life and times of the Holmans. What about you? Tell me about your family."

He bit into a roll and chewed extra slowly.

She watched him with interest.

"You have to swallow sometime, Jack. What deep, dark secrets are you hiding about the Stinson family?"

He finally swallowed. "No secrets, deep or dark." He shrugged off her comment. He was being honest. There are no secrets. He simply didn't want to talk about his family, but he sure couldn't expect her to share family information with him and not return the favor. He wouldn't mind telling her all about his mother and his brother, Eric. But he knew she'd expect to hear about his father and he wasn't in the mood to discuss him. Right now, he'd rather just avoid the subject of his dad altogether. "I'd much rather hear about you as a scrawny pig-tailed little urchin."

"How did you know I was a scrawny pig-tailed little urchin?" Her head tilted in curiosity.

"The pictures around your home, for one thing. I especially liked the one of you sitting in the cockpit with your black felt cowboy hat and no front teeth. Charming."

She tossed a roll his way. "There *are* pictures around the house of me with teeth. Did you notice any of them? And, I still have that hat in a closet somewhere if you'd like to borrow it."

"No thanks. It looked better on you."

"Okay, so you've seen me at my best. Now tell me, Jack." She gave him a stern look. "As your boss, I demand to know. What was life like for Jack Stinson near the big cities of Dallas and Ft. Worth? Were you a serious kid or is that a recent development?"

He considered her question, knowing she wasn't going to let the interrogation rest. "Was I a serious kid?" He never thought about it that way. "Yeah, I guess I was. I mean, I think I was a typical kid, but our family was quite a bit different than yours. We didn't tease each other like ya'll do. My dad was and is a strict disciplinarian."

She nodded her understanding.

"You know where Cryder is, right? Outskirts of Ft. Worth. Since you're big on short versions, I grew up there, graduated from high school there, graduated from college near there, went to work for my father, and now I'm here. That's it." He avoided her eyes, slipping another bite of roll into his mouth.

"Sounds like a good life." Her voice was sincere. "Stable."

"You know, you're right." He had to chuckle at the irony. She wanted what he had; the part about working with his dad, anyway. And he wanted what she had. If they could have changed places though, he was certain the work she longed for would not seem nearly as attractive to her. Their fathers were total opposites.

"Has Felicia or your other sister shown any interest in flying?"

She tilted her chin at him. "Nice subject change. But let's finish this one before we start dissecting my life again. I'll bet you left a dozen broken hearts behind."

He shook his head and smiled at her question. "No time for that, remember? And besides, you're being nosey."

She threw a grape at him. "Of course I am. Now, talk."

"Hailey, don't. That's childish."

"Of course it is." She aimed another grape at his face.

"You'd better stop wasting food."

She fired the grape at him, and he opened his mouth just in time, catching the grape between his teeth.

She clapped her hands and laughed, plucking another grape. "What are the chances of doing that again?"

He issued her a stern warning. "No!"

"Oh, alright, Mr. Starched Shirt." She reached for the napkin in her lap and wiped her fingers.

"That's *stuffed* shirt. And thanks."

"You're welcome. I'm just glad you can admit it."

They ate quietly for a moment before Jack broke the silence. "Ok, your turn. How about you and this Brently—"

"Bradley," she corrected with a full smile. "He liked my black cowboy hat."

"I'm sure he did."

"Honest!" She held her hand up, palm facing him as if taking an oath. "We loved each other a lot, still do, but we weren't *in* love." She shrugged. "Like I told you before Brad said adios Barnes. Hello big city life. Which is fine. I'm so glad he's happy."

"So, you two are still friends. That's good."

"Of course. Since we were in diapers as a matter of fact, and we always will be." She retrieved a slice of jalapeño pie. "But just think, not being involved in a serious relationship has given me the chance to focus on the business. I wasn't kidding when I told you I haven't had time for much of anything else."

He tipped his iced tea goblet to his lips and then set it down. "That's right. Miss One Track Mind."

"You make being focused sound like a case of the flu. And you're obviously one to talk."

His father's driven face flashed through his mind. "Not the flu. Just a bad head cold. Or bronchitis, maybe." He laughed at his own wit. "Pretty good, huh? For a stuffed shirt."

She chewed the bite of pie in her mouth and raised her hand to high-five him.

He slapped his hand to hers. "No business should consume your life. Believe me, I know. You have to have fun to balance the work."

She swallowed and speared another bite with her fork. "My work is fun."

"You know what I mean. We all need diversions. Something different."

"You're right, Jack."

"Because I finally hit the wall and realized my life was so out of balance that…*what* did you just say? I'm *right*?"

"I wondered when you were gonna catch that." She laughed. "I agree. Balance is good."

He was actually surprised and thrilled by her quick admission. "Exactly! Sure, I'm focused on work, but the way my dad drives everybody around him is ridiculous. There's a point where you can get obsessed."

Her eyebrows rose. "Define obsessed."

"Alright." He didn't take her cue to stop while he was ahead. "I want it all, not just a successful work life. I want a big hound dog thumping his big fat tail against the floor because he's so happy to see me get home from work every day. And a good woman who loves me. Someone I can love forever. And kids. A mortgage and a boat. I've always wanted a boat. I've just never had the time."

"You sound obsessed with having it all."

He leaned closer to her. "I am." He smiled.

She returned the smile.

"Let's get back to 'you're right, Jack.'"

"Did I say that?" she teased.

"Yes, ma'am. When I said we all need diversions."

She nodded at his words. "Don't you think my mom is diversion enough for anyone? And we won't even get into the whole Neal and Paul thing."

The lightness in her voice made him crinkle his brow. He decided to re-voice the question that kept tugging at his mind. "But, how can you say you have so much respect for your dad and so little for your mom?"

The joking glint quickly dimmed. "Please don't say that, Jack. I'm doing this as much for her as I am for myself and my dad. And for my sisters, too. My mom will never come to terms with Dad's death until she comes to terms with the business."

"Somehow there's a compromise that would allow both of you to be happy. Maybe you're just not seeing the whole picture."

"Giving up flying completely is the only thing that will make her happy." *Lord, help him understand!* She plucked a grape from the stem and put it into her mouth. Then she took a bite of cantaloupe.

"You don't think that maybe you're being a bit selfish?" He knew the second he said it. It was a bad idea.

She couldn't chew and swallow fast enough. "Am I the one being selfish? She's the one who's tried to stand in everybody's way. She's the one who's always tried to stop our dreams. And that's like…like breaking a bird's wings and leaving it to suffer and die!"

Her direct, piercing words echoed through the empty loft.

He wanted to say he understood what she was saying, because in a way, he did. He knew all too well. But still, he couldn't help but wonder about Rinnie Holman's deeper motives. Reason told him there was more to why the woman was so adamantly opposed. Nobody in their right mind acted this way without a shred of reason.

Oh, well. Of course. His dad's face flashed before his eyes again and reminded him that, yes, some people do in fact act that way. Even if no one can figure out what their shred of reason might be.

Jack reached for his tea.

A sudden thump against his chest brought his full attention back to her face. He stared in open disbelief. "You hit me with another grape." He retrieved the grape that had fallen beside him on the quilt and placed it on the side of his plate. "I can't believe it. We're in the middle of a deep, serious conversation, and you do something so…so childish."

"I'm not being childish. I'm clearing the air."

"You never give up, do you?"

"No, I never give up. You'll learn that." She picked several grapes and held them in her hand.

He shook his head. "I guess I already have."

Well, that's just fine, he thought. Two could play this game. He reached for a slice of cantaloupe. "So I guess that means prepare to meet defeat, Miss Holman."

"I'm not worried." She let the grapes fall from her hand back onto her plate, holding empty palms for him to see. "You're too much of a gentleman to attack an unarmed lady."

"Unarmed? As long as you have that mouth of yours, I hardly think you're unarmed."

She pretended to take offense, but then gave him a confident smile. "I'm not worried. Like I said, you're a gentleman."

"That's right. I'm a gentleman." His teasing mood slipped from his fingers with the cantaloupe he returned to his plate. He reached across the quilt for her hand, accidently brushing the candles between them. Two hot flames hit the quilt. Jack grabbed his iced tea goblet and doused the small blaze before it could spread. Hailey swatted at the smoking material with her linen napkin.

He frowned at the charred blotch on the quilt. "I really am sorry, Hailey. I'll have this replaced."

She fingered the material. "I can patch it. I'm just thankful we stopped it." She motioned to the dry straw that filled the loft. "It could have been much worse."

He sucked in a deep breath. It certainly could have been much worse. "I really do apologize."

She offered him a half smile. "Things were getting a little heated, I suppose. But don't worry about it. God's got everything under control."

Jack searched the smiling face before him. Was she talking about the fire? Or his attempt to kiss her? The God he knew watched from His throne and hit people on the head with a powerful rod any time they stepped out of line. In his mind, a kiss wasn't even close to misbehaving. "You mean, God doesn't like for us to have fun down here on earth, so He stopped me from kissing you."

"Kissing? We weren't kissing." Realization crossed her face and she stifled a grin. "God doesn't zap us if we try to have fun. That's not what I meant at all. And there's *nothing* wrong with kissing, but come on. You and me...if we had kissed just now, it would have changed things between us. And neither of us wants that. Right?"

He hesitated. "You won't consider letting me even kiss you? Just a simple kiss?" His voice was earnest.

"You're definitely kissable." She seemed surprised by her own admission. "But neither of us wants to complicate things, do we? I sure can't afford that kind of distraction, and I don't think—deep down—you need that either right now."

Her words hit a familiar nerve. *Distractions*. That word again. His father hated distractions, too. Work, work, work. No time for anything else. What was he thinking? Hailey Holman was every bit as bossy as his father.

And unfortunately, she was certainly bossing her way right into his heart.

CHAPTER ELEVEN

After the barn incident, Hailey and Jack worked at keeping their time together strictly business.

It wasn't easy for Jack, since her presence was proving more and more to be a challenge to his heart. He knew he was getting a little too close. In his eyes, she didn't have a clue how interested he actually was. And he had to admit, her resolve was impressive. Frustrating, but impressive.

Rinnie Holman was still civil. Mostly. And he woke up surprised every day that he was still here working with Hailey after four weeks. He had to start making calls to find another job. Soon.

One good thing was the Watson boys' outbursts were loud but so far harmless, just like Hailey promised. And the work was more than rewarding.

Then Hailey approached him one morning with a request that tested the boundaries of his benevolence.

"You want me to do what?"

"Babysit. Just watch little Dee for me."

"You want me to babysit?"

She eyed him as if her request was perfectly natural. "Yes, Jack. Just for a few minutes. Dee's a great kid."

"She's a great kid, yes. But I can't be responsible for a small child." Jack knew his protests fell on deaf ears. He'd be stuck babysitting this little girl no matter how hard he fought it.

"I'm sorta in a bind, Jack."

"Nothing personal against Dee, she spends a lot of time around here, and she's definitely about as well-behaved as a little kid can be," he added. "Not that it's rocket science to keep an eye on a six-year-old, but it's not in my job description, so no. No!"

"Oh, Jack, stop being dramatic. An hour, tops."

"No. I'm a mechanic, remember? Not a babysitter. This isn't a place for children to play. It's dangerous around the hangar. All the tools she could get into…"

"What do you suggest, then? That I send her back to her house? Carleen's working the morning shift at the diner, and I sure don't want Neal and Paul pretending to watch her."

"Then take her with you." His voice was somber. The last thing he wanted was for Dee to go back to her own house to be with those drunkards. But the next to last place he wanted her was stuck there with him.

Hailey persisted. "I would, and I usually do, except this morning I have an appointment for a check-up and my mom's already gone into town for a meeting. Ms. Carleen didn't plan on working this morning. One of the other waitresses called in sick. And besides, Dee wants to stay here with you. She likes you."

He held his hands up in a hopeless gesture.

Hailey tossed him an understanding look. "Listen, Felicia only has one final to take this morning, so she'll be home soon, and Mom shouldn't be too long with her Friends of the Library meeting. Just hang in there for an hour." She patted his shoulder before turning to leave. "You'll be just fine."

"And you wonder why I'm still gonna start looking for another job," he called after her. *At some point. Soon.*

She waved at him and continued around to the garage. "You're a big help, Jack. Now get back to work." Her playful tone drifted back at him.

Jack watched as Hailey pulled her truck around and down the gravel drive, making a right turn and heading in the direction of town. Then he turned his attention across the yard to the little girl who'd been left in his charge.

Dee jumped from step to step across the back porch, brownish curls bobbing around her head.

What was he supposed to do with her? He'd never been around kids much. What if she had to go potty and asked for his help? At six? No, probably not. He supposed he could pour apple juice and fix a bowl of Cheerios if she got hungry.

He allowed a confident smile to ease across his face. Kids were kind of like miniature people, he reasoned. And Dee really was a likeable little kid. Spunky. Probably something like Hailey must have been when she was younger. If he stayed around much longer, it would be okay to spend some more time getting to know the little kid. He wanted kids someday. Maybe four. *Hailey would be a great mom.* He shook the thought off with a vengeance.

Stop thinking like that. He watched Dee chase a butterfly and he let out a deep sigh. Okay, this is the hand he was dealt and it would be fine. He just wished he knew more about what watching a child on his own entailed. Some warning would have been good. Not being thrown into the full care and responsibility of a little human being at a second's notice.

Jack watched her hop to the bottom step and gather up some crawly creature from the ground. What *would* it be like to have a child of his own? He quickly chastised himself. Hailey wouldn't even kiss him, so how did he suppose she'd consent to marry him and have babies?

The thought brought a crimson scowl to his face and he turned on his heel to march back into the hangar. The heat must be getting to him, he decided, fiercely resenting the way his own brain put thoughts in his head that were never going to happen. *She's told me enough times.*

Jack threw himself back into his work, anxious to escape the uninvited thoughts rolling around in his mind. It was clear Hailey viewed him as nothing more than an employee. How many times did she have to remind him? A *temporary* employee, he should toss back at her. A mere distraction. *That's what she called me. A distraction. Man, if that doesn't beat a guy's ego, nothing will.*

With a vengeance, he slipped a nut over the end of the bolt beneath the wing. *And what do I care, anyway? It's best for me, it's best for her. It's best for everybody. I don't need feelings like that murking up my life. Like Hailey always says: Bad timing.*

"I'll just keep my distance from her. That's what I'll do. And that little bundle of energy bouncing around playing across the yard? I'd better not get too attached to her, either. I'll definitely keep my distance. Hailey had better be right about her mom and sister returning soon. The sooner the better," he muttered to the plane.

Jack busied himself with his work and before he knew it, over half an hour had passed. He craned his neck to see through the double doors of the hangar. No Dee in sight. Good. Felicia or Mrs. Holman must have returned and taken the little girl inside. They should have told him they were back, though.

He returned his attention briefly to his work. But a nagging concern for the little girl made him decide to check, just to make sure.

Hopping down from the wing, Jack plucked a towel from the workbench, wiping his hands as he stepped into the open doorway and scanned the backyard. Tucking the towel into his back pocket, he walked around to the front of the house.

He glanced in the garage. No cars. Maybe she was around the side playing with Kisses. A hurried look told him she wasn't there, either.

There was no one around except the scattering of livestock gathering on the other side of the fence.

He cupped his hands around his mouth. "Dee? Dee! It's Jack. Where are you?"

With no response, a ripple of panic started in his stomach. He wanted to kick himself for letting the child out of his sight. He knew kids needed to be watched. She was more important than whatever work he'd accomplished on the plane.

He strode hurriedly around to the front of the house. Maybe she had gone into the house for a drink. Maybe he'd find her sitting in front of the TV watching a square yellow sponge cartoon or those talking vegetables she liked to watch.

He stepped onto the porch and Kisses, who had been dozing in front of the door, rose to greet him. The dog's thick tail beat against the side of the storm door.

"Hello there, Kisses." He patted the dog's head. "Seen Dee lately, fella?" He pulled on the door handle and stepped inside. His eyes adjusted from the bright sunlight to the dim quiet living room. "Dee?" he shouted into the house. "Dee!"

No answer met him, just the whirl of the air conditioning unit kicking on.

He stepped out and closed the door behind him, calling her name as he made his way across the porch and back down the steps. Kisses followed at his heels. "Where could she be, boy?"

Jack's eyes searched the fields beyond the front gate. "Dee! Answer me!"

The same dead air met him. He patted Kisses on the back. "Stay here, boy. I'll find her."

He made his way through the gate and headed back toward the rear of the house. Where in the world could she be? Surely her dad couldn't have driven up without him noticing and taken the little girl. No, he'd have heard that rattly old pickup. And Kisses certainly would have alerted the entire county of the unwelcome presence.

Maybe…his mind raced and a glimmer of hope filled him. Just maybe she'd gone out to that old flatbed trailer to play. *That's where she has to be. I'll probably find her sitting on the rope swing, laughing and bouncing those little curls of hers.*

Now a surge of hope pushed him forward and he found himself racing to the shady spot in the pasture where Hailey and Dee had taken him. The secret hiding place. He was sure glad she hadn't kept it a secret from him.

Reaching the flatbed, his heart sank. No sign of her. He turned a complete circle and scanned the grassy pasture. *Okay, God, this is what You do, right? You help lost people?* He cupped his mouth again and shouted into the air.

He was about to turn to leave when a tiny voice called out.

"Help. Jack?"

The muffled plea came from beneath the trailer. He fell to his knees and peered into the low, darkened space. A tightness gripped his chest. "Dee!"

"Jack." She sniffed loud. "I thought I had to be under here forever. My hair got stuck. It's so hot under here! Jack, help. Pleeeease."

He breathed a sigh of relief. "Thank God…thank goodness you're okay." His eyes focused on the little girl. Sure enough, from what he could make out, her hair was somehow wrapped around something beneath the trailer. The tightness in his chest intensified. "Can you reach up and unwind your hair, Dee?"

She burst into tears.

"Okay, okay, maybe not." He surveyed the situation further. "You just hang on, Miss Dee, I'm going to take care of everything." He stood and grabbed onto the side of the trailer. "Dee, I'm going to lift the side up a bit and you tell me if you can undo your hair, okay?" This had to work.

A shaky *"okay,"* drifted at him from beneath the flatbed. He positioned both hands on the trailer, but knew instantly that he'd never be able to lift even an inch of what had been welded by time and the elements into the rock hard ground. He dreaded telling her. "We're going to try something else, Dee. I'll have you out of there soon."

"Okay," And then he heard her begin to sob again.

"Dee, why are you crying, honey? I'm here to help you. I promise I'll get you out!"

"But you're mad at me. I cry when people get mad."

"But I'm not mad. You didn't get stuck under there on purpose, did you?"

The tiny voice issued a weak "No."

"Well, see then. No one will be mad at you. We'll all be so happy to get you out of there. So, see. You don't have to worry about anything."

"Jesus wouldn't be mad." Her voice was no longer shaky. She sounded adamant. "He wouldn't be mad for me gettin' stuck under the trailer. He'd just come and find me and take me back to the house and let me play with Rena Wayne."

"Who's Rena Wayne, honey?"

"My baby doll that Santa brought me when I was little. Jesus would let me play with her when I get back to the house."

Jack's heart heaved. She made it sound so simple. Like it was a fact and nothing could change it. He didn't know how to respond to such innocent assurance. "I suppose you're right, Dee."

"It sure is hot here, Jack. I feel kind of sick. And I can't hardly breathe, neither."

Jack didn't hesitate further; he plopped down flat on his belly and shimmied himself across the hard dirt under the trailer. Reaching her, he squeezed her sweaty little hand. "You're right. It's too hot to play under here today, Dee. Let's go back to the house."

She tried to nod her head. "Ouch. That hurt." But the sound of her voice was suddenly stronger, and that was music to his ears. He let go of her hand and went to work.

He unwound her hair from a piece of the metal frame beneath the trailer and slipped his hand back around hers. The two wiggled from beneath the trailer. Reaching the end, a reviving breath of air hit their faces. Jack sat on the ground and propped his arms across his knees.

Dee threw her arms around Jack's neck and plopped into his lap. "Thank you for saving me, Jack. You got me unstuck!"

For a moment, he was taken back by the demonstration of gratitude, but then a slow smile eased across his face and he hugged her in return. "I'm glad I was here."

Jack held her at arms' length. "You're sure you're okay?" He looked at the curls that were now drenched ringlets around her head and the red, swollen and dirt-streaked face.

She nodded. "I'm real good. And it's a good thing me an' Hailey showed you our secret hiding place, huh, Jack?" Her red-rimmed eyes were now shining.

He returned her nod slowly. "A really good thing, Dee."

He gave her back a pat and lifted her to stand on her feet, then he pushed himself up to stand beside her. "We'd better get back to the house. Mrs. Holman or Felicia might be back by now. And they'll be wondering where you are."

She grabbed for his hand and began swinging their linked hands back and forth happily.

"Okay, Jack. Let's go!"

He scooped her up instead and cradled her in his arms. "How about I carry you to the house. That way you'll feel better. We can get you a nice cool drink."

Dee smiled her agreement and nestled her head against his chest. "Apple juice."

"Apple juice." He assured her. "Coming right up."

His feet began moving in the direction of the hangar, but a startling thought drew his mind back to the shady spot beneath the big oak tree. He turned his head to look over his shoulder.

Climbing under that trailer had been tough for him. Tougher than it should have been. His heart was still racing. What was that? Fear?

Fear? Of what?

The realization washed over him like a tidal wave. Tight places. Smothering.

He'd never wanted to feel the suffocating tightness that had plagued him for the past several years. The four walls of his office had closed in on him until nothing was left except the boxed in feeling of panic. He hadn't wanted to feel trapped that way, ever again.

That's outrageous, he told himself with a long shake of his head. Downright ridiculous. *Those words again.*

The thought jolted him. *Downright ridiculous.*

He looked down at the curly headed little angel snuggling in his arms. She'd helped a fear surface he didn't even realize he had. And helped him conquer it, all at the same time.

She smiled up at him and he returned her smile, tightening his grip around her. "You're safe, Dee," he assured her.

Right now he felt freer than he had in years. He'd call his mom after work this evening to thank her for her prayers. Something like peace was beginning to settle over him. He wanted to share that with her. *She'll be so happy for me. Maybe she'll see that I really am okay, and will stop worrying about me.*

His eyes scanned the cloudless sky. He suddenly felt the need to know how his father was doing. And how Eric was getting along. It was time to face and conquer many of the issues he'd shoved aside.

What was it that Dee said? Jesus would find her and save her and take her home. He squeezed her tightly again. "Come on, Miss Dee. Let's go home."

CHAPTER TWELVE

"Could this mean that big sister has finally found Mr. Right?" Lindsey Holman poked her sister in the ribs, obviously enjoying the scarlet hue creeping up into Hailey's cheeks.

"Ok, Lindsey Lou, you can go back and spend the weekend at the dorm if that's the way you're gonna act." Hailey plopped a handful of ice cubes into the final glass and began filling glasses with sparkling brewed tea.

Lindsey slung an arm around Hailey's shoulders. "Felicia was right, big sis. I caught a glimpse of him through the window. He's gorgeous!"

She shrugged away from Lindsey. "Caught a glimpse, my eye. You spied openly without shame." A good-natured thread of accusation ran through her voice. "You're not mature enough to understand this, my dear, but it is possible to be friends with someone of the opposite sex without romantic involvement."

She issued Felicia a warning "you promised" glance. The disastrous makeover was history. There was no reason for anybody to get the wrong idea. Or for her image to be spoiled. That foolishness certainly wasn't going to happen again. The divas could keep their Plum Passion lipstick and helmet head hair spray.

"Ewwww. Romantic involvement." Lindsey swiped a carrot stick from the tray Felicia prepared. "Now that sounds promising. You have a way of making it sound so perfunctory."

"Perfunctory. Big word college girl." Hailey showed her sister a playful snarl. "Behave."

"Oh, I'll behave myself at dinner. In front of your," she popped the last bite of carrot into her mouth "boyfriend."

"Business colleague." Hailey hoped she sounded as nonchalant as she attempted to feel.

The truth was, she'd been praying for strength where Jack was concerned. Romance. Not in the plan. Closed case. Her heart just needed a little nudge to be reminded once in a while.

A light knock on the back door caused her to issue one last warning to each sister before hurrying to open the door for Jack.

Dee rushed in past him. "I'm starving hungry!" She didn't stop to acknowledge anyone's presence as she raced through the kitchen and into the hall toward the bathroom. "I know, wash my hands," she called on her way through.

Jack smiled his hello and took a step into the kitchen, catching the heavy storm door before it could slam shut. "Smells good in here."

"Mom's chicken salad." Lindsey drew in a satisfied breath and let it out before rubbing her tummy. "Boy, do I miss her cooking while I'm gone. I am *not* taking another semester of summer school. I'm staying home."

Hailey totally understood. "I used to feel the same way when I was away at school." She set the glasses filled with tea down on the table and then turned to Jack. "Jack, this is my sister Lindsey." Hailey's smile visibly threatened her sister. "Lindsey, meet Jack. My business colleague."

Jack extended a friendly hand. "Nice to meet you."

"And it's *so* nice to meet you." She took the hand he offered, but cast an obvious glance at her older sister. "I've heard so much about you, *Jack*."

Before Lindsey could mortify her further, Hailey discharged an order. "See what's keeping Deedles, please, Lindsey. You know how she likes to play in the water."

Jack held a chair out for Hailey. "Where's your mom? Isn't she joining us?"

"Tonight's her Garden Club pot luck. She worked on a fund raising project most of the day, came home, cooked and went back. She fixed enough for all of us."

"Yeah," Lindsey returned to the kitchen with Dee in hand, and seated herself across from her older sister. "I'm sure they're having more than twenty different types of Jell-O salads and five bean casseroles. Yum."

Dee hurried to the table and stood beside Jack. She grabbed him by the hand. "I want to sit by you."

"Good." His smile was genuine. "I want to sit by you, too."

She scooted two chairs close together and hopped onto the nearest seat.

Felicia and Lindsey exchanged amused looks. Lindsey leaned across the table to whisper to Hailey. "Don't be zealous, now."

Hailey scowled and mouthed "I'm warning you" at each of her sisters.

"I'll say the blessin', okay, Hailey?" Dee's eyes sparkled as she waited for Hailey's nod.

The little girl squeezed her eyes shut and folded her hands under her chin. "Dear God, thank You for all this good food and for lettin' my friend Jack save my life and for Hailey and Lindsey and Felicia and Granny Rinnie and my grandmama and for Kisses. And thank You, too, for lettin' me stay here. And thank You for my daddy and let him be better. Amen. And thank You. Again."

A twinge of humility flickered in Hailey's heart. *Lord, forgive me. Help me to be kinder to Neal and Paul.* Her eyes rose to meet Jack's eyes. He gave her a slight knowing nod.

As the plates were served, Dee launched into another recount of the morning's rescue. No matter how Jack tried to shift the conversation, she repeatedly focused the attention back to him, much to his growing embarrassment. Hailey found herself enjoying the increasing redness of his cheeks.

The group had finished their meal, cleaned the kitchen, and settled down to play a game of Monopoly when Rinnie returned from the potluck dinner. She stood scowling at the front door for half a minute and then without a word to anyone retreated down the hall to her bedroom.

Lindsey shook her head and gathered her play money along with the property she'd acquired. "What have you people done to her while I was gone? She looks like she's so mad she could spit hornets."

She turned in her assets and cash. "I quit," she said, collecting the steamboat token she'd been using to mark her place. "Carry on without me. I'll go talk to Mom."

Hailey nodded and continued with her throw of the dice.

Jack watched her. "Let's call it a game. I think you need to talk to your mother, too."

She moved the miniature iron six spaces. "Jack, you know there's nothing I can do right now." She counted out several bills from her wad of colored money. "I'll buy St. James Place, thank you very much."

Jack put his hand on top of hers. "I think you should go in and talk to her."

"Lindsey is. They haven't seen each other for over a month." Her face softened. "Listen, it hurts me, but I can't do anything right this minute. Lindsey coming home is the best thing for her right now. I'm putting on my strong face." She leaned toward him with a deep forced smile. "See?"

Felicia turned in her money and property. "I don't feel like playing anymore, either. I think I'll go to my room and just chill out." She turned to Dee, who was busy arranging hotels and houses along an imaginary road she'd constructed on the shiny hardwood floor. "Come on, Dee, let's listen to my new CD."

The little girl jumped up and threw her arms around Jack's neck. "Bye, Jack. I love ya'." She threw herself at Hailey. "I love ya, too, Hailey."

And then she grabbed Felicia's hand and tugged on it, smiling up at the teenager as she led her down the hall.

Hailey smiled after them. "I think you've found a lifelong friend." She slipped assorted money denominations into the appropriate slots.

Jack cleared the board and folded it, placing it back into the box to put away. He rose. "Yeah, I guess I have. Think your mom will ever be my friend? Or is there just going to be a big wall of animosity toward me? It would make a great deal of difference."

She cocked her head up at him. "How?"

He fit the top back on the box and set it down on the coffee table. "What do you mean, how? Everyone feels the anger in the air around here. How can you be so casual about it all?"

The old defensive tug of war seared through her heart. "How can you say I'm casual about my mother's feelings? I'm not, and you know it."

"Well, I'm telling you there's much more to this than simply your mother's dislike for the business. It's deeper than that, and frankly, it irritates me that you can't—or won't—see it."

Her eyes burned and the years of listening to her dad try to reason with her mother came through her mind. "Are you judging me, Jack?" She tossed her head. "I hired you to do a job and to do what my father would have had you to do. Not to sit here and criticize the decisions I have to make. I've told you from the first day how much my mom's disapproval hurts. And I don't ever— *ever*—want to hear you criticize me for doing what I have to do again."

Her breathing slowed, and she kept her eyes focused on his face. What was he thinking? *He sits here facing me with such calm disapproval. I can hardly bear it. Not from him, too.* The thought tore at her heart.

"Jack, I love my mom so much, and you should understand that by now. But I can't be the little ballerina she'd hoped for. I can't be the obedient little bank teller, or the pianist, or the librarian or whatever. No matter how much I love her, I can't do it. From what you've told me about your dad, you of all people should understand."

"Yeah, you're right. If anyone should understand it, it's me. And I do to a point. But I'm telling you, your mother's motives are deeper than what you know. I can't believe for a moment that this gracious woman is simply bitter about the time and danger involved in flying. She doesn't strike me as that type of person at all."

He stretched his hands toward her, offering to help her to her feet. She hesitated, not willing to admit that maybe, just maybe, she might need his help for more than just working on the planes. And she wasn't just referring to getting up off the floor.

She finally allowed him to pull her to her feet, and they walked in silence to the front porch. She settled herself in the middle of the closest swing. The surprise that filled her when he scooted himself in beside her nearly took her breath away. "There's a perfectly good swing over there, Mr. Stinson."

"I like this one better." He folded his arms across his chest. "How far are you going to carry this?" he finally asked quietly.

She gave the swing a push with her foot, avoiding his question. "I told you my dad had a heart attack." She shivered slightly in spite of the evening's warm stillness.

"Yes. You told me."

Her mind burned with the memory, but she suddenly wanted him to know more. Maybe then he'd realize why she had to be firm in what she was doing. "I hadn't been back at school for very long that semester. Dad was the one who had insisted I go back to get my degree. It was hard for him when I left, but he insisted. Without me here to help him, he worked double to stay caught up. He sat in his recliner one evening after supper and went to sleep." Her blurry eyes stared straight ahead. "He simply went to sleep."

"I'm so sorry, Hailey." He touched her shoulder gently. "You can't think your being gone had anything to do with it."

She shook her head softly. "I know. I know." A lump caught in her throat. "He'd gotten to fly earlier that day, though. Shouldn't that be some consolation? That one of the last things he did was what he loved best? I have only two regrets."

"Which are?"

"First, that I wasn't with him on his last flight."

"And second?"

She ran a hand along the heavy metal chain that held the porch swing. "That I wasn't here when he actually closed his eyes for that last time. Maybe I could have done *something…*"

"Don't do that to yourself. There was nothing you could have done."

"Oh, I know. But there is something I can do now." She turned to gaze into his eyes with thoughtful introspection. *Understand Jack. Hear me. Please.* "Families do what they have to do to support each other. My dad could have given up flying a million times, but what would that have accomplished? We are all responsible for our own attitudes, and giving away a part of your heart and soul to make someone else happy is not the solution to any problem. The problem here isn't the planes or flying. The problem is control. And an unreasonable fear that she can't seem to let go of. It would have been wrong for us to give in and let her fears control all of us. Maybe your situation is different, I don't know. I love my mom, even though we have this…this wall hanging between us. But I can't abandon myself. All I can do, Jack, is love her."

He nodded his effort at understanding as she continued.

"I respect my dad for who he was, and for me it's a comfort knowing that he's in heaven now, soaring with the angels."

"I wish I could take the pain away." He leaned his face closer to hers, his voice tender with emotion.

"I didn't plan to involve you in anything more personal than working on the planes. But it just…happened." She trapped her lower lip between her teeth. "My dad gave his life to this business. He gave his life so that I could come back and take over." The pain of missing him stabbed at her heart. "Do you see why I'm so bull-headed about it?"

They sat together, the question unanswered, swaying gently in the swing, neither breaking the stillness of the dark, windless night. Hailey let the whisper of the porch swing's creaking lull her heart back into a steady rhythm.

She finally sighed. "I've sat here hundreds of times, Jack. Praying that Mom would come around. That's why I know…" Her eyes scanned the star-filled sky. "That's why I know—"

Before she could finish, Jack leaned toward her and pressed his lips gently to her forehead.

It was an innocent enough gesture, but Hailey's thoughts disappeared somewhere into the darkness, and her heart pounded hard against her chest. She kept her eyes focused straight ahead.

Lord! I'm normally so in control. I'm the one who always takes charge. And then he had to enter my in-control world. I've always known what I want! But now…it was just a little kiss.

But it spoke volumes to her heart.

"I'd really better be going inside now." She heard a quiet voice that sounded familiar yet far away. It surprised her to realize it was her own voice. She'd behaved strangely since this man arrived at her doorstep. Blushing, smiling more.

"I'd better be going inside now," she repeated.

He spoke solemnly. "You said that already."

"Then I suppose I meant it." She stood up with a jolt, leaving him in a gently swaying swing all by himself. She closed the door behind her and leaned back against the hard wood of the door. She touched her forehead gently and then touched her fingers to her lips.

"Goodnight, Jack Stinson," she whispered into the empty living room. She squeezed her eyes shut. *Lord, keep me from being distracted. Keep my attention focused on what You will have me to do. Help me get myself back together. Please.*

Then she locked the door and made her way quickly to her bedroom.

• • •

Jack entered the cottage and closed the door behind him, heading straight for the telephone. He picked up the receiver and punched in the numbers with quick efficiency.

Maybe he shouldn't have done that. He certainly hadn't planned it. But he wanted to. He knew now that he'd do anything to stay near Hailey. To help her.

A familiar voice answered on the other end of the line, and he lowered himself to sit on the end of the sofa. "Hello, Mother."

At the sound of his voice, the woman on the line let out a warm laugh. "Oh, Jack, my dear one. It's so good to hear your voice. You sound good."

"You sound great yourself, Mother."

"Jack, tell me how you're doing." She lowered her voice. "Are you doing all right, dear? I had a feeling you were going to call tonight."

"I'm really doing very well." He wanted to get right to the heart of his call. "Mother, how is Father doing?"

"Your father…well, your father is doing fine. I just hope, Jack, that you don't feel resentment toward him. He had a difficult time growing up with your grandfather. He's the way he is because he was raised that way."

"I think I'm beginning to understand that now."

The surprise in her voice was evident. "Good. Good, I'm glad. Always remember, Jackie, your father loves you very much. We must always try our best to understand each other, especially family. He may act like a tyrant, but you know, he does love you and your brother."

"I know." He'd already been given the understanding each other speech tonight. He missed his brother more than he realized, and he hoped leaving hadn't caused Eric a bunch of stress. The last thing Jack wanted to do is take stress off himself, only to put it on someone else. "How is Eric?"

His mother let out a laugh. "Managing your father a bit better than you did, I'll admit. Eric knows how to step around Father's moods. He'll do just fine, I'm thankful to say."

"I'm glad." He let out a relieved breath. "I did the right thing in leaving, Mother. It was the best thing for all of us."

"I agree, darling. You have your life to live. If you'd stayed, I'm sad to say, Father probably never would come around. I miss you terribly, but it's enough just knowing you're happy."

She hesitated. "You are happy, aren't you Jackie? I hope you've found what you're looking for."

He hesitated. Peace and fulfillment was what he was looking for. The events of the month tumbled through his mind and he couldn't help but smile to himself. "I may not have totally found what I set out for. But then, I may have found even more than I was looking for." *But that's a discussion for another time.*

"Mother, may I speak to Father?"

The silence on the other end seemed deafening. "Why don't you wait a bit longer, dear? Just until Marshall's had a chance to come to terms with your leaving. Just a little more time will make a world of difference. He misses you, I know. But you know his silly pride."

"All too well, I'm afraid."

"Someday soon, Jack. It would be better if you'd talk to him then."

As Jack said goodbye to his mom and returned the receiver to its cradle, an overpowering urge to see his father came over him. He could no longer allow anger and ego to stand between them.

What was it Dee said? Her words still rang in his ears. Something about how Jesus wouldn't be mad. From the mouth of babes—"*and the little children shall lead them.*"—The thought popped into his head; from where, he didn't remember, but he knew he'd heard it somewhere.

If only he could recall some of those Bible stories he'd learned as a child. They never seemed to pertain to him before. They seemed as remote as the good childhood memories he tried to remember.

The thoughts running around in his memories were confusing and at the same time, comforting. How far should a person go in carrying out their father's will?

That was something he suddenly felt he had to learn for himself.

CHAPTER THIRTEEN

Swaying in the swing her dad made, enjoying the comfort of the porch he'd built, Hailey closed the Bible in her lap.

A smile touched her lips. This was the best part of the day. *I love it when I can get up early and have the beginning of the day all to myself.*

Her quiet time was especially good this morning. She'd gotten up even earlier than usual and settled herself on the front porch swing, sipping hot raspberry herb tea and reveling in her quiet time. She certainly felt calmer than she had the night before.

She reached down to run a gentle hand through the hair on Kisses's back. "Hey old boy. Sleepy head." It was an added comfort to have her dear friend snooze at her feet. "Lazy dog," she chuckled. "What'd you do? Stay out all night last night chasing fireflies or patrolling the property for stray cats?" She tousled his head. "Okay, sleep then, lazy bones. But tonight you're going to bed early."

Hailey rose from the swing, stepping over the big pile of chocolate colored dog. Tiptoeing back through the living room and to the kitchen, she set her Bible on the counter top and rinsed her tea cup, setting it in the sink. A little spark of excitement made its way through her.

She walked from the sink to the back door. *I'm not gonna be uncomfortable about that friendly little show of affection.*

She let the heavy storm door close behind her and started down the back porch steps. It was going to be another scorcher, no doubt about it, she knew that already.

Last night was last night. Over and done. Today's a brand new day. She paused to gaze up into the cloudless blue sky.

There was nothing as peaceful as the clean freshness of a brand new day, especially one when she hadn't had to face her mom's unhappy face yet.

She stole a look at the cottage as she tread up the yellow brick pathway. As peaceful as it looked outside, she could imagine what it was like inside. Jack must be scurrying around readying himself for work. Probably just now shaving. Or rolling up his shirt sleeves. She shook her head softly. *Oh, good grief. Gotta stop thinking about him.*

She turned her face away. Silly putting so much into a simple kiss on the forehead. *He's probably thinking no wonder Mark went into the priesthood.*

Okay, Lord. Remember what we talked about this morning? You and I decided to put last night behind me and push forward. And You're going to help me.

She stopped before the hangar doors and gave herself a good mental shaking. *I am glad that I told Jack more about my dad. Because now he understands my determination. Maybe we'd even work as more of a team. Like dad and I were. The Blue Yonder Flyers.*

With a wide smile tipping her lips, she reached for the hangar doors and pulled back the latch that held the doors secure.

Flinging the doors wide, she let out a gasp that sucked every ounce of breath from her body. Hailey felt as if someone had punched her in the stomach with a bowling ball. Her knees buckled and she caught herself against one of the doors. The scene before her eyes was way beyond her wildest comprehension.

Someone somehow had taken something and smashed her planes to death.

Supporting herself against the door, Hailey struggled to find her breath.

She didn't hear Jack coming up behind her.

"Good morning, boss…" His voice trailed at the sight of her face. He walked up beside her, gaping in amazement at what he saw. "What in the—"

Hailey barely heard him. She looked at one windshield, smashed but still hanging in the frame like a million microscopic spider webs. The rudder was ripped completely off, and the door leading to the cockpit now bore deep pits as if it had been crushed with a sledge hammer. It was now nearly impossible to read the carefully scripted lettering on the side of the Skycat III through all the damage.

Jack touched her shoulder. "Hailey."

She brushed his hand aside numbly and wheeled around to face him, beating her clenched fists against his chest. "Tell me you don't know anything about this."

Tears found their way to her stunned eyes and her whole body shook uncontrollably. All reason escaped her and she lashed out at the closest target. "Why? Why?"

He eyed her in astonishment. "You can't possibly think…" He grasped her firmly by the shoulders. "Hailey, listen to me. How on earth could you think I even remotely had anything to do with this? I've given you no reason to even suspect…this is ridiculous!"

She twisted her body from side to side, writhing to free herself from his grip. "I don't want your hands on me. I don't want anything to do with you!"

"What? Hailey—"

"Get away from me! Do you hear?" She spoke through teeth clenched so tightly that searing pain raced through her jaw. "I want you out of here and don't you ever come near me or my aircraft again!"

He struggled to hold her still. "Stop it," he commanded. "Stop it right now and talk some sense to me."

She kicked at him. "I'll never forgive you. Let me go and get off my property or I'll have you arrested."

He dodged her angry kicks and pulled her tight against him to stop her struggles. "You're going to listen to me, do you hear me, Hailey?"

One foot connected with his shin bone and he grimaced, tightening his grip on her. "You're something else, you know that?"

She sucked in a shaky breath and stopped struggling. "Let me go." If her voice was venom, he would have dropped dead where he stood.

He refused to loosen his grip. "No. I won't let you go. Not until you listen to me." He examined her face. "I don't know what happened here, but I'm not responsible for it," he stated firmly. "Why would I do something like this? I have no motive, not an inkling of a reason."

She stood glaring at him, her jagged breath escaping through clenched teeth. "I don't know. Why would you?"

"Think about it. What would I gain? In fact, I'd be out of a job, now wouldn't I?"

"No. You'd be more needed than ever."

He dropped his hands from her shoulders and propped them on his hips. "You beat all I've ever seen, do you know that?"

Her gaze remained steady on his. "It's the only explanation I have right now." She fought the urge to beat on his chest again. "You're the only logical choice. You and—" She shook her head from side to side.

"Say it," he demanded. "Me and?"

"You and my mom."

He raised his hands in disgust. "Now I know you've lost it." He paced away from her in exasperation and then turned back to face her, drawing a handkerchief from his pocket. "Here." He held it out to her and she reluctantly took it. "Can we talk rationally now?"

Holding the handkerchief against throbbing eyes, she shook her head. "No. No, I can't be rational. Dad's planes…" She felt the panic boil from the pit of her stomach and she trembled as she looked at him. "My poor Dad."

A muscle in his jaw tensed. "You know who did this, don't you? It was those Watson boys."

She shook her head. "No. It couldn't have been. They were my first thought, but…but I ruled them out pretty quickly." She wiped her eyes. "You know how Kisses goes crazy whenever they're around. I would have heard something."

He surveyed the damage from his position at the hangar door. "Who in the world would have done something like this?"

"I thought maybe…well, it entered my mind that, maybe you were…" She threw her hands up in irritation. "Oh, I don't know. It doesn't make much sense now that I think about it."

She took a closer step toward him and let her head fall against his chest.

"Actually, it makes *no* sense." Jack was pensive for a moment before putting a protective arm around her shoulders. He stroked her hair. "Don't worry, Hailey. We'll find out who did this. We'll find out."

"Jack, I have to face facts." She raised tear filled eyes to his. "I know in my heart who did this. And it hurts to even say it, but I suspect it was my mother."

"Absolutely not. You can't even think it. Your mother would never do anything so violent. This is something a crazed psycho would do."

"Normally, I'd agree. But how many times has she said she'd do anything to keep me from flying again? She's gone too far this time, Jack." She flashed her eyes at him, but this time the anger she felt was fused with pity. "And it's going to take more than I have in me to ever forgive her."

"I do not believe it, Hailey."

"Think about it. She's been behaving so coldly toward you. She's desperate to keep me from reopening the business. Kisses would have barked if a stranger had been prowling around last night. Especially Neal or Paul. We both know that."

"And you didn't hear barking or growling or anything all night? You're positive?"

"No. Not a peep."

He clasped her arm firmly. "Come on, we're going to get something straightened out right now. And then we'll call the sheriff and let him find out who did this."

She wasn't sure why, but she allowed him to lead her from the hangar doors, along the yellow brick road and to the back door.

She didn't even try to stop the tears. Or the hurt ripping through her heart. Down to the pit of her stomach she felt sick. The last thing she wanted right now was to look at her mother. *I want my dad. Oh, Father, help. Set things right. Help my mom. She's lost it. Please.*

Hailey was suddenly grateful for the strong arm leading her up the back steps. How could she have lashed out at him, thinking he'd done it? *I'm grateful for Jack. I really am.*

•••

"Mother, I have something to say to you." The suffocating tightness in Hailey's chest made her stop to catch her breath. This was almost too much to endure.

Jack took a step toward Rinnie, who sat at the kitchen table, running a needle and thread through the hem of a white lacy apron. She glanced up, a scowl on her lined face.

"Mrs. Holman, Hailey has some disturbing news. It seems that some time during the night—"

"Somebody busted up the planes," Hailey interrupted, her arms crossed rigidly across her chest. "And I think you had something to—"

Jack placed a steady hand on Hailey's shoulder. "Mrs. Holman, did you hear any strange noises last night?"

"Mother," Hailey shoved Jack to the side and recrossed her arms.

"*Hailey!*" The outburst from Jack turned her head, and she opened her mouth to speak but closed it again.

Rinnie tied a knot in the thread and bit the end off with her teeth before folding the apron calmly. She set it on the table and rose to her feet. "I don't have to listen to this. I'm weary of the whole mess. I told you it was a big mistake to reopen this business, but you wouldn't listen."

Hailey's face fell. Her mother's calmness was the last thing she expected. As her mom walked stiffly from the room, she turned to face Jack, anguish resurfacing in her eyes.

"What did I tell you? She all but admitted she did it." She gave her head an unbelieving shake. "Can this really be happening? I feel like I'm in the middle of a horrible nightmare, and no one will awaken me."

She ran trembling fingers through her bangs. "I can't believe this."

Jack puckered his lips in annoyance and shook his head. "I don't know. The whole thing is too strange. I still don't believe it."

"Well, believe it."

"She was just so calm."

"Sure she's calm, Jack. She took all of her frustrations out last night while she was smashing up the planes."

"No, Hailey. I'll admit her reaction is a bit strange. She doesn't seem surprised at all. Like maybe she's even…"

"Glad?" Hailey finished his sentence. Do you think I want to believe it? I don't! But I do believe that my mother…"

"Don't say it anymore. Just take a deep breath and let's think this through. I know you're in shock."

"Yes! I am in shock, Jack. My own mother." She choked on a sob. "Where did all that rage come from? She's ill, Jack. We have to get her help." Pain rippled through her. "To be opposed is one thing, but to actually…I never saw it coming." She sank down onto one of the kitchen chairs. "I never saw it coming."

"Like I said, we don't know that it was her, Hailey. For one thing, how could she have the physical strength to do that much damage? That took a lot."

"Heard of adrenaline? If she's that desperate, she'd be able to move this house if she wanted to."

"Well, whoever did it—and I'm not saying that I'm at all convinced it was your mother—certainly wanted those planes out of commission."

Hailey's jaw tensed and she narrowed her eyes at him. She banged a determined fist on the table. "Maybe she did put us out of commission." She stood and leaned firm palms across the tabletop. "For the time being, anyway. But this is not going to stop me."

CHAPTER FOURTEEN

"What do you mean, 'For the time being?'" Jack felt his blood pressure rise.

"You don't really think this little stunt is going to stop me, do you? Whoever did do this has underestimated me." She straightened her back and lifted her chin. "I suppose you haven't known me long enough to know better than that. But my mom certainly has."

"Exactly! She'd know this wasn't going to stop you. She'd know it would only make you more determined than ever. Why would she risk that?" He didn't like the determined gleam spreading across her face.

"Hailey, I can certainly understand your hostility. But we need concrete facts before we accuse anyone of what went on in that hangar last night."

Frustration shook through her body before she abruptly moved toward the door.

Jack stepped beside her, reaching out and clutching her by the arm. "Wait."

"Don't try to stop me, Jack."

Her voice held more pain than anger now, and he resisted the urge to pull her to him. He was painfully aware that he couldn't shield her from what she was going through. His mind scrambled for words to help her understand. "You know, you keep talking about all this 'calling' stuff."

"Don't start on me," she closed her eyes. "Not now, Jack."

His mind continued to fight for something he could say that would get through to her. "It seems to me that with your mother so dead set against a flight business, you'd at least question your 'calling' theory."

Her expression dropped and she opened her eyes. "What? That *again*? Just because my mom never respected my dad's dreams doesn't mean I should step aside and let her destroy everything he worked so hard for. It's my responsibility to—"

"Your responsibility? Is that how you look at this, Hailey?"

"I'm going to do what's expected of me." Her voice was firm, final.

"'Responsibility. Expected. You sound like a vigilante when it comes to this business."

"Stop it! You're as ridiculous as everybody else around here."

"Well, I'm not the one who's put pretty much my entire life on hold so I can finish something that someone else started, regardless of how everyone else feels."

"You stop it. You don't know, Jack. This is—"

"Your calling."

"Yes!" She screamed the word at him.

"Then where was God when this was going on last night?" his voice rose to meet hers. "Where was God when your mom was begging you to let it go? Where was God when your dad's dreams weren't realized?"

The questions lunged from his lips without warning.

She opened her mouth in total disbelief. "I can't believe you said that. Don't you dare blame God for this. He doesn't force His will on us. We're not puppets. He doesn't control our every move." Her voice was barely a whisper.

The agony in her eyes pierced his heart. *How do I respond to her?* He kept his mouth shut.

"I choose to do His will because I love Him, Jack. And I love my dad. And the best way I can honor that love is to continue the work my father began."

He released her arm slowly. *Maybe she's right about us not being puppets.* A shadow of comprehension touched his face. *With all her heart she believes in what she's doing. With all her heart she loves her dad and loves God.* "You really believe that God wants you to resume the business." It wasn't a question.

"Of course I do. What have I been telling you and everyone else?" Her voice was definite. The emphatic light in her eyes punctuated her resolve.

He took in a deep breath and offered her a slow nod. "Alright, then." He let the air out of his lungs in one steady release. He let his eyes mold to hers. "Again, I'm with you. I can't believe I'm doing this. But we'll find out who did this. We'll get help for your mother if she needs it. We'll work things out with her. We'll see what we can do about the Watsons. We'll work through the obstacles. Together."

She seemed uncertain at first, soaking his words into her heart. Then she nodded her agreement. "I don't know what to say. I don't know why you're agreeing, after everything, but…I really do appreciate you, Jack." She gave him a grateful look. "I can't believe you're going to hang in there with me." She shook her head. "You came here expecting something a whole lot different, and you've hung in through some craziness. I'm not going to question why, I just know I'm thankful."

"You don't corner the market on hopes and dreams, Hailey. I'd like to see this work, too. But be realistic. You may have to concede on a point or two. Or three even." He raised his eyebrows at her. "You can't just go through life bulldozing your way through others to get where you want to be."

It was evident his words stung. "Is that what I do? Bulldoze people?"

"In a way," he chose his words carefully. "In a way, you do. Your heart is in the right place. Your father would be proud of your determination in his name. But you can't be so all-fired set in doing this that you forget the people around you, the people who are still here. The ones who need your love and commitment, too. Isn't that a part of God's will for all of us? Is this business the sole reason God put you on this earth?"

Hailey closed her eyes and let her head fall back. "Sometimes…" Her voice trailed off and she raised her head and opened her eyes to look at him. "Sometimes I've felt like it." Her voice was soft. "I just want to do what's *right*."

"Look," Jack began calmly. "If your mother is the one, don't you think she's going to need all the support we can get for her? It would mean she's disturbed. Not just a little bit, either."

"You're right."

Her prompt admission took him back. "Yes, Hailey, and I'm not being glib or anything like that this time. I am right on this."

Before Hailey could respond, a tearful Dee suddenly appeared in the doorway, her hair tousled and her face drawn. She stood facing both of them. "Hailey, don't be sad." She began to sob. "Don't be sad."

Jack hurried to scoop the little girl in his arms. "Hey, nobody's sad. What are you doing up so early?" He patted her back softly as she lay her head on his shoulder.

Hailey stepped toward them and smoothed the little girl's hair. "Shhhhhh. It's okay, Deedles. Go back to sleep. Everything's gonna be okay, sweetie."

"You were crying." She picked her head up from Jack's shoulder. "I heard you. And yellin', too."

Hailey kissed the top of Dee's head. "You don't have to worry, baby. Everything's fine." She smiled. "Do you want Jack to tuck you back in?"

She nodded against Jack's shirt. "I didn't barely sleep none last night." She yawned, and her eyes closed before Jack could tiptoe back to lay her in the day bed in Felicia's room.

When he returned, Hailey had her purse on her shoulder and keys clenched in her hand.

"Let's drive over to the diner. I think it would do us both good to get away from here for a few hours and I need to talk to Uncle Frank."

"Are you sure we should leave, Hailey?"

"I'm sure. If it's my mom you're worried about, don't. She's either back in bed or waiting until we leave to come back out."

He cast her a concerned glance.

"It's okay," she assured him. "Dee won't get up again until Felicia does. Lindsey will sleep until noon. Trust me on this one. Come on. Will you drive?"

He nodded and hurried back to the cottage to retrieve his keys. Trust her. That's exactly what he wanted to do. But…his stomach was beginning to hurt.

• • •

The first face to greet them at the diner was Carleen Watson. She made her way toward them with a smile and a steaming pot of coffee in her hand. "Hey, kids!" she called across the tables to Hailey and Jack. "Let me pour these boys over here some caffeine, and I'll be right with you."

Hailey nodded her acknowledgement.

Jack noticed an ample man with a huge shock of gray hair glance up from the cash register where he was breaking a wrapper of new dimes into the drawer. He smiled and nodded his head as Hailey motioned to a booth in the far corner of the room.

"We'll be over here, Uncle Frank," she called above the chatter and clanging of dishes.

"Where's Aunt Shirley?"

"Just back from the bank, kiddo. I'll tell her you're here. We'll be 'round to say hey in a sec."

Hailey nodded and led the way around the close quarters filled with square center tables, each one topped with different colored plastic. They reached the last of three bare wooden booths lined against the back wall. She slipped in and slid her purse strap from her shoulder, clasping her hands tightly in her lap.

Jack slid in across from her. "Nice little place." His eyes canvassed the room. Movie posters adorned the walls. James Dean and Natalie Wood stared into each other's eyes. One showed Doris Day and Rock Hudson in a serious lip lock. But it was mostly John Wayne who plastered the walls. The picture above their booth announced a movie named *Stagecoach*.

The man from the cash register bustled over and sat heavily on the bench next to Hailey, bestowing a mighty hug around her neck.

Uncle Frank caught Jack's interest. "That one." He jabbed a finger in the air at the direction of the old poster. "John Wayne's big breakout role."

Jack's admiration was evident. "Really? That's interesting."

Uncle Jack's head bobbed up and down, "Yep, big role. *Ringo*! You a fan?"

Jack nodded. "Yes, sir. Who doesn't like The Duke?"

"That's what I always say." The older man slapped the table and delivered a huge grin Jack's way. "Now, Shirl," he motioned with his head toward his wife. "She likes this tear jerkin' movie stuff. So she's got her favorite movies around, too."

He turned his attention to his niece. "Comet, girl, what brings you 'round this time o' mornin'?" He tipped his Texas Rangers cap at Jack and held out a thick calloused hand. "Better introduce myself official. Frank Richard. Or Uncle Frank around here." He poked a playful elbow at Hailey's side. "Right, sug?"

Hailey made an attempt at a smile. "I'm sorry. This is Jack Stinson, Uncle Frank."

"Sure, I know who this young man is." He shot Hailey a knowing look before smiling back at Jack. "I've heard all about ya."

"Uncle Frank, I need to talk to you. And to Aunt Shirl. It's serious."

"I can see that, sugar." Uncle Frank turned his head to scan the room, catching the eye of a petite woman with big-rimmed glasses and short graying hair. He waved her over. She waved back and began moving toward them, pausing at each table long enough to issue a greeting to the breakfast crowd.

When she reached their booth, Shirley Richard stretched to lean past her husband and planted a kiss on the top of Hailey's head.

Jack slipped out of his polished wood bench seat and stood waiting to be introduced to another of Hailey's relatives.

"Girl, what are you doing in town this early? Hey, you been crying? Feuding with your mama again, huh?" Then she turned to Jack, acknowledging his presence. She grabbed his head and pulled it toward her, kissing the top of his head, too. "And this is your pilot friend, I guess." She held out a hand covered with silver rings on each finger for him to shake. "Hello, pilot friend. Don't tell me your mama refused to feed you kids this morning. That gal's got some mad on about all this work you two are doin' on those planes. Let me get a coupla menus."

Hailey cast a pained look up at Jack before turning her attention to her aunt. "No. It's a lot worse than that, Aunt Shirl." She fidgeted with the silverware rolled tightly in a paper napkin in front of her. "Do you have a few minutes to sit with us?"

Shirley shot her husband a questioning look, but nodded her head. "Well, sure, baby. We've got all the time in the world for you, you know that." She slid across the seat and folded her hands on the table in front of her as Jack settled beside her.

Before Hailey could begin, Carleen scooted up with a tray of cups and saucers, and a pot of fresh coffee. "Can I get you good folks somethin' to eat?"

Hailey shook her head. "We have a real problem, Ms. Carleen. You're welcome to stay and hear about it, if you want. You'll hear about it anyway."

Carleen glanced across the diner. "Freida! Cover for me, please." And then she pulled a chair from a nearby table to sit at the end of the booth.

Jack surveyed the sweet, dimple-faced woman sitting with them. It didn't seem feasible that she could be the mother of those trouble-making Watson boys.

Hailey relayed the morning's catastrophe to the group amid gasps of disbelief and astonishment. No one agreed with Hailey about Rinnie's involvement. Ms. Carleen sat quietly, shaking her head, while Uncle Frank watched his niece with concern.

Jack thought from the look on Ms. Carleen's face, she had to be thinking the same thing he was thinking. And it wasn't a good thought.

"Come on, sug, you know your mama isn't capable of doing something that mean spirited." Uncle Frank kept his eyes on Hailey's face. "You know it as well as we all do. She's got a stubborn streak in her, just nearly as wide as your daddy had. And you, of course. But mean, no ma'am."

Aunt Shirley agreed. "After all these years, darlin', she's not gonna do anything to harm those planes. She's been through it all with your daddy."

"I don't know." Hailey rubbed her finger across a deep heart-shaped scar carved into the wooden table. "She's unreasonable when it comes to the business and those planes, you all know that. Why can't she just get over it and let me do what I have to do?"

The look between Uncle Frank and Aunt Shirley seemed lost on Hailey. But not on Jack.

The rivet of concern that crossed the table spoke volumes to him, and he knew for certain then. He'd been right all along about Rinnie Holman. There was something more Rinnie Holman didn't want to share with her daughter. Something he was determined to find out for himself.

Jack reached across the table and grabbed Hailey's hand in his. "I'm going back to the house. You stay here with your aunt and uncle."

She opened her mouth to protest, but Jack was already standing beside the booth with his Jeep keys in his hand. "I'll be back to pick you up in an hour or two." He nodded to the group. "It was nice to meet all of you. I only wish it could have been under more pleasant circumstances."

Hailey tried to scoot her uncle from his place on the seat. "I'm going with you, Jack."

"No. You stay here. I want to talk to your mother. Alone." He turned to make his way across the room.

She was adamant as she called after him. "You will not. This is my battle!"

He stopped and turned back to face her. "This isn't a battle, Hailey. It's time you learn that."

The only thing Jack heard as his hand touched the door to leave the diner was her Uncle Jack's deep voice boom above the commotion in the diner. "I think you've met your match there, Miss Comet." He was chuckling with obvious admiration. "I think you've finally met your match."

CHAPTER FIFTEEN

When Jack appeared in the doorway, Rinnie Holman was sitting in the kitchen with her two daughters and Dee, eating eggs and toast. "Girls, the cows need feeding."

Lindsey looked like she wanted to say something but thought better of it. "Yes, Mom." She lifted Dee from her seat at the table and helped Felicia set the breakfast dishes in the sink.

Both girls gave Jack a stunned "do you have any idea what you're doing?" look before obediently heading for the door.

It surprised Jack that Mrs. Holman so readily agreed to speak to him alone. He was prepared to have to talk her into it.

She led him into the living room and sat rigidly on the sofa, crossing her hands in her lap, her expression painfully blank.

Jack settled across from her in the leather recliner, leaning toward her and resting his arms across his knees. "Mrs. Holman—"

"I know Hailey thinks I did it," she interrupted.

He held his eyes steady on her face. "Yes. She does."

"Well, I can't help what she thinks." Her frustration was evident. "I'm sorry if her heart is broken, but she'll get over it. She'll mend." Her soft hazel eyes looked directly into his own. "I've had to many times."

"What do you mean by that, Mrs. Holman?" His tone was sincere.

She sucked in a deep breath and let it out slowly, seeming to choose her words carefully. "Mr. Stinson, I believe, in spite of the circumstances of your arrival here, that you may be a fine young man. But you should mind your own business. My daughter loved her father deeply. She thinks that airport will keep him alive forever." She unclasped her hands and let her palms rest lightly on her lap. "It won't. He's gone. And she can't carry on for him."

"You do know that Hailey feels that God has called her to carry on for him."

The corners of the older woman's lips curled up and Jack saw the tiny lines that crinkled around her eyes. "Yes. She feels this is her calling. But Mr. Stinson, God doesn't expect her to live Web Holman's life for him. He wants her to live her own life."

"She feels this *is* her life. But what about you, Mrs. Holman? Are you telling Hailey everything she needs to know to help her understand your feelings? Is there anything else, something more in the past that could help her discover if she really is following God's will for her life? Or is it simply a desperate attempt to be loyal to her dad…" He moistened his dry lips. "Especially when she feels that you haven't been."

She seemed to stare past him. He continued cautiously.

"I can't help but feel that your motives are deeper, Mrs. Holman. It's not just that flying scares you, is it? I think maybe you have more reasons to feel the way you do. Reasons that Hailey knows nothing about. Maybe if you confided in her, she'd be able to understand—"

He halted as the smile left her lips and a dark cloud shadowed her face. "Some things are best left alone."

"Not if knowing could bring understanding."

"It's okay if my daughter thinks I destroyed those planes. I'd rather she believe that and hate me forever instead of…" She stopped, avoiding his eyes.

"Instead of what?" He wasn't letting her off the hook that easily. Hailey needed to know why her mother objected so fiercely to the business. She deserved to know.

"That's all I have to say to you or to anyone else about this matter, Mr. Stinson." Her voice was firm but suddenly kind. "Let it alone. Please."

He let her words sink in before rising to his feet, offering her a slow nod. Understanding washed over him. He was wrong to have told Hailey that he'd stay. He wanted to. But he suddenly knew it wasn't the right thing to do. They both had life-changing things to work out. He had to do it his way. And she'd have to do it her way.

"Mrs. Holman, I respect you enough to think that you must have a good reason for disliking flying and the business as much as you do. I just wish you could tell Hailey what that reason is. It could mean the difference between an estranged life for the two of you and letting a whole lot of healing into your lives."

He turned to leave but then shifted back to face her. "I don't know if you played a part in what happened last night or not. I doubt you did. But for Hailey's sake, I'll see to it that she no longer blames you. Tell her I did it, if that's what you want, but let her know that you love her and that you're here for her. You've both lost someone you loved very much and whether the two of you realize it or not, you need each other. Hailey's lost her father. She doesn't need to lose her mother, as well."

Jack let the heavy storm door close securely behind him, and made his way down the porch steps and along the gravel drive to the cottage.

Kisses jumped at his legs, begging for Jack's attention. He smiled sadly and patted the big chocolate colored dog on the head. "Take care of our girl, Kisses."

He walked on with Kisses trotting along beside him. When he reached the cottage, he patted the dog's head one last time. "Go back to the house, Kisses. You're needed there." He pointed, fighting the ache that tore through his heart. "Go."

The dog's reluctance to leave touched him. Maybe he'd have a big chocolate colored Lab himself, someday. "They love you, no matter what," he murmured softly.

He took the first step up to the porch, and stopped, turning to peruse the open sky. His mind soared with a distant recollection.

"He loves us, no matter what." He marveled at the words. "God loves us. God loves us. No matter what."

He'd never said the words aloud. He'd never thought much about the validity of the words he'd heard as a small child. No matter what he'd done. No matter what his father had done. No matter what Rinnie Holman had done—or not. No matter what Hailey harbored in her heart. No matter how evil Neal and Paul Watson acted…He loved them.

Jack recalled his own mother's words to him the night before. "We must always try to understand people's motives."

He'd never get to the bottom of Rinnie Holman's objections, that was evident, but he hoped someday Hailey would. The one thing he could do now was work to discover his own father's hidden fears.

Why, Jack wondered, had it been so important for him to help Hailey understand her mother when he hadn't even tried to understand his own father? Maybe his father thought he had justified reasons to drive himself—and his family—to work harder. There was only one way to find out.

Jack turned the doorknob and walked into the well-crafted, love-filled cottage. Hailey might shift the blame for the planes to him after he left. Wouldn't it be as much as an admission of guilt for him to up and leave without notice, especially after he'd already agreed to stay? That might be good. He knew Rinnie wouldn't take him up on his offer to shoulder the blame. But no matter what happened, the relationship between mother and daughter had to be restored.

Jack reached for the yellow note pad and pen by the phone. He sat heavily on the chair and put pen to paper. It hurt knowing he told her he'd be here to help her through. But God would explain everything.

• • •

Hailey held the folded yellow paper in her hand. "What is this?"

Lindsey shrugged. "Jack said to give it to you. That's all I know. I didn't want to read your mushy old love letter."

"I can assure you that it's not a mushy old love letter." She unfolded the note and read the first few lines. Her eyes burned. She held the paper to her chest. "How long ago did he give this to you?"

Lindsey checked her watch. "Thirty-five, maybe forty minutes ago. He said to pick you up here at the diner and give you this note."

Hailey grabbed her sister by the arm and ushered her through the door. "Take me back to the house. Fast."

Lindsey did as she was told, pushing the speed limit a bit more than usual in the process. When they arrived home, Hailey bolted from the car and raced straight to the cottage. Out of breath, she burst through the door. She knew instantly she was too late. He was gone.

She took slow steps back to the porch and flopped herself down on the top step. Opening the yellow piece of paper and reading the lines again, her heart began to ache.

> *Dear Hailey,*
>
> *By the time you read this, I'll be on my way back to Cryder. In our hearts, we both know it's best if I leave. You've taught me a great deal in the short time we've been together. You've made me realize that it's never wise to run from our place in life. But first, a person has to determine where that place is. I have things to work out with my father. And you have things to work out with your mother. I believe you may even have unfinished business with your own father, Hailey. Settle it. Do yourself and your dear family a favor: forget about the planes for awhile. Understand each other first. Love each other. It will all work out. I promise you that.*
>
> *Love,*
> *Jack*

She ran a hand through her bangs and attempted to sort the confusion racing through her brain. No, he couldn't have wrecked the planes. Or did he? Maybe that's why he left. But that made no sense. It made even less sense to have blamed her mother, though. Rinnie wasn't a violent person. There were just too many questions. Too much confusion.

Hailey buried her face against her knees. *Help me to understand. I feel angry and helpless.* She blinked at the tears stinging her eyes.

Why did he desert me? Couldn't he see how much I need him? How dare he…how dare he…

Her head jerked up and she gasped as the realization slapped her squarely in the face: *Am I talking about Jack? Or my dad?* She let her head fall back on her knees and struggled to grasp the thoughts chasing each other around in her mind.

"Hailey, let's talk."

The soft voice startled her and she looked into the weary hazel eyes of her mother. She nodded vaguely and scooted to make room.

The two sat in silence for a moment, both staring out across the horizon, until Hailey cleared her tightening throat. "Mom, I think I've accused you falsely." She barely spoke the words.

"No, Hailey." Her mother reached for Hailey's hand. "You haven't. I may not have physically damaged those planes, but I've prayed for something, anything to happen to keep you from flying again."

"Dad told me. That you were in a plane crash. I thought you should stop living your life in fear and stop trying to put your fear on us. I wanted you to see how God had taken care of you." She turned tear-filled eyes to face her mother.

Rinnie touched a soft finger to her daughter's cheek, intercepting a tear that spilled. "Before I met your father…" Her voice trailed away and she took a deep breath before continuing. "Before I met your dad, I was married to another man."

"Mom!" The shock hit Hailey full force. "How could you have kept something like that from me all these years?"

"I've never told you girls because," Rinnie squeezed Hailey's hand and stroked it lovingly, "it was such a big, big mistake. Sometimes children make the same mistakes their parents have made. If you'd known that I was once a divorced woman, then divorce may have become more acceptable in your eyes. It wasn't an option I wanted you to think you had. It wasn't something I was proud to tell you."

"I can't believe it, Mom. I can't see you as divorced. I mean, I understand people make mistakes, and divorces do happen, but… mostly I can't believe you've hidden it from us all of our lives." Her eyes grew wide and the words threatened to stick in her throat. "Did Dad know?"

Her mother nodded. "Yes, of course he knew. I married at seventeen because I had hoped having one less mouth to feed and body to clothe would help your Gramma and Granpa."

"That's no reason to marry." There was no judgment in her voice. "Did you even love the guy?"

"I suppose I did. He was my high school sweetheart." A frail shudder encased her. "You know, when he proposed I thought it was an answer to prayer. Your grandmother raised us kids to believe that God would always take care of us. I truly thought marrying him was what God wanted me to do." She looked deep into Hailey's eyes. "That's how easily we can misunderstand God sometimes."

Hailey bit her lip and lowered her eyes.

"Hailey, sometimes it's hard to know what God wants you to do. And other times it seems to be written across the sky in giant letters."

Hailey returned her gaze to her mother's face. "What happened, Mom? Why did you divorce?"

Her mother seemed resigned. "He'd always been so kind to me. That was before he started drinking and staying out all night with his GI buddies. It didn't take me long to figure out I wasn't to question his whereabouts, either. The first time he hit me, I was so terrified. I'd never been treated like that before."

"Mom, I'm so sorry. That's horrible." She regarded her with somber curiosity. "I understand about the crash. But I don't understand what any of the rest of this has to do with me. Or with Dad. Or flying."

"A few weeks after the divorce was final, I learned I was expecting a child. I had nowhere to turn."

Hailey clutched her mother's hand, the blood draining from her face. "I'm not…I mean, I couldn't be…"

"Oh, lands, no, Hailey, absolutely not!" She gave her a reassuring pat on the knee. "You are Web Holman's daughter beyond a shadow of a doubt."

The relief on Hailey's face was immediate. "Then what happened? To the child, I mean."

"A couple on the base where we were stationed in Pensacola took me in. Then your Uncle Frank and Aunt Shirley offered to let me live with them, so I boarded a plane and they were to pick me up in Houston." Rinnie's hand trembled at the recollection. "There was a technical problem on the plane and that's when we made a crash landing. Twelve people died and I lost the baby. At the time I wished I'd died, too."

Shreds of understanding began flooding Hailey's heart and compassion swept over her like a tidal wave. "Oh, Mom, I'm so sorry. I wish you'd told me."

"It seemed best not to. How did I know that you were going to fall in love with flying and planes like your father? I tried my best to discourage him—and you—but as you see I failed miserably."

Hailey threw her arms around her mother and held on tight. "Oh, Mom, you didn't fail. I was the one who insisted on having my way." She released her grasp on her mom and covered her face with her hands. "It took a stranger to see that there was more to your motives than—"

"Than zealotry and selfishness? And maybe some spite? And irrational fear?" She raised her eyebrows and Hailey offered an apologetic nod.

"I'm sorry, Mom. Please forgive me. I feel so selfish." She blew out a deep breath. "I've been so convinced this was God's will for my life. It seemed the only way to truly honor Dad. I miss him so much."

"My darling daughter, you've given your father the most wonderful honor. You'll always be his flying buddy. His little Comet. No one can take that away from you. Not me, not anyone. But don't think you have to replace him, either. You cannot replace him."

Hailey wiped a tear. She didn't trust her voice to speak.

Her mother took both of Hailey's hands in her own. "Now you listen to me. That young man was willing to take the blame for what someone else did so you could have some closure. He was more concerned about you being okay than anything else. I'm not absolutely certain who did it, but I have my suspicions." Rinnie stiffened her back. "All I know is, Neal and Paul are the only two scoundrels around here low enough to do something like that. I don't know how, but they'd be my first suspects."

"That's what I thought, too, but there's no way they got past Kisses. I guess instead of grabbing at straws trying to make sense of who, I should have called Sheriff Maxey right away." She laid her head on Rinnie's shoulder. "I was angry with you, Mom. I think I wanted it to be you so I could feel better about going against your wishes. I thought I was going to have to fight you for the rest of my life, and that felt horrible. I *knew* that was wrong. But I just wanted dad's dream…"

Rinnie smoothed the hair back from Hailey's face. "Darling, I know, and I understand, how important the business is to you. I think it's because it's a part of your dad and you want desperately to hang on. But I know your father would agree. It seems you may have someone else to hang onto now. And if you don't go after him and set things right, it'll be something you'll regret for the rest of your life. And believe me, I know about regrets."

Hailey's heart felt torn in half. If she left to see Jack now, while the airplane matter was unresolved, she'd be letting her father down.

What would best honor him? "Mom, what would Dad want me to do?"

"He'd want you to be happy."

Hailey bowed her head in prayer. It was time to ask God what *He* really wanted her to do. And for her to finally *listen*.

CHAPTER SIXTEEN

Hailey slipped an extra pair of jeans into her suitcase and checked one more time to make sure she'd packed her toothbrush. She flipped the top and pulled the zipper closing around the ends of the bag.

She turned, suitcase in hand, to find Dee standing in her doorway wiping at red eyes with the hem of her sundress.

Hailey's mouth curved into a sad but affectionate grin. "I'll be back soon, Deedles. Don't cry." She set her case down and stepped forward, giving the tiny girl a full hug.

"I'm not cryin' cause of that." She wiped her eyes on Hailey's shoulder. "I'm cryin' cause of my daddy and Uncle Paul breakin' up your planes."

"Sweetheart, we don't know they did it." She knelt eye level to Dee. A twinge of guilt tugged at her heart. How much had Dee overheard this morning?

But Dee's curl's bobbed. "Uh-huh. 'Cause they were here last night."

"Are you sure, sweetheart?" Her stomach roiled. Part of her brain knew it had something to do with them, but a small part still wondered. "Did you hear Kisses barking last night?"

She nodded again. "For a bitty minute, but then they gave him something to eat. I saw them. And then Kisses went really to sleep and didn't say nothin' to them. I saw them."

Hailey bit her lip. So that's why Kisses seemed groggy this morning. They drugged him! Still, it was beyond her comprehension that Kisses would take food from them, or that they could even get close enough to give him food.

"Please, Hailey. Please don't be mad cause I didn' tell you this mornin'. I was 'fraid you'd be even madder at my daddy and Uncle Paul. You're always mad at 'em." She sniffed hard. "You always don't like 'em."

Hailey closed her eyes and buried her face in Dee's hair. She had decided to pick and choose which of her father's traits to honor, and mercy toward the Watson boys hadn't been one of them. "It's okay, baby. I'm not mad at them anymore."

Dee pulled away from her in wide-eyed wonder. "You're not even mad at 'em for breakin' Papa Web's planes?"

Hailey shook her head slowly, standing and stroking Dee's hair. "No, sweetheart. We're going to get Papa Web's planes fixed." She felt a tug of forgiveness, for the boys and for herself settle into her heart. "And we're going to get a whole bunch of other things fixed, too."

"Can I tell Felicia and Lindsey?"

Hailey's mouth curved with tenderness. Was there anything as pure as the love and innocence of a child?

She grabbed Dee up in a grand hug and kissed her on the nose before setting her back on her little bare feet. "You bet! You can tell them all about it."

Felicia appeared in the doorway. "Hey, little gal, your daddy's waiting in the driveway for you."

"Can I tell him, too, Hailey?"

Hailey straightened her shoulders and sucked in a deep breath. This would take more strength than she knew she had. This would take God.

"I think I'll tell him myself. How would that be?"

Dee's fair curls bounced around her head in an enthused nod.

Before turning to leave, Hailey reached into the top drawer of her vanity and pulled out an unopened sack of chocolates. She placed it in Dee's hand. "This is all yours. Now go tell Granny Rinnie you're leaving. And I'll walk out and speak to your daddy."

Dee bubbled her thanks, and Hailey turned to take steady steps to the driveway, a silent prayer filling her heart.

Yes, it was definitely time to get a whole bunch of things fixed.

• • •

Neal Watson leaned his tall lanky frame against the rusty pickup, seemingly preparing for the worse as Hailey made her way through the front gate. He muttered something she couldn't hear to his brother, who waited inside the ragged cab.

Neal tipped his cap briefly, avoiding her eyes. He eyed the suitcase in her hand. "Runnin' away?"

Hailey shook her head. "No. Just going to take care of some important business." She walked to her own truck and set her suitcase into the back. "We need to have a little talk, Neal."

"Ya know I'm always happy to talk to ya, neighbor." His eyes seemed to drink her up.

She chose to ignore his lewd expression, returning his stare with solemn concentration. "I'm holding you responsible for the damage to our planes."

He opened his mouth to protest, but before he could respond, Paul yelled out from the passenger side of the pickup. "We didn' do nothin'! You can't say we did, neither."

Neal tipped his cap back on his head. "Oh, shut up, Paul!" He turned his attention back to Hailey. "I'm not admittin' nothin', you understan', but if I was, how'd you find that out? About us, I mean."

"I kind of fooled myself at first. But I can see clearly now." She took a step closer to him and he leaned back harder against his truck.

"We haven't been very nice to each other, have we, Neal?" Her heart swelled with unexpected forgiveness. In her eyes, the boys didn't look evil and mean anymore. They looked pitiful. Scared. Like frightened little boys who bully others because they don't know any other way to make themselves feel worthy. "And Neal, I'm sorry about that."

He cocked his head at her. "Why would you be sayin' somethin' like that to me? We've given your papa and the whole county a whole buncha grief. Why'd you be so nice to me, now? It's a trick, ain't it." he said flatly.

"No, no trick. But I think it's time we all grew up and stopped this ridiculous fighting. You and Paul. Me. It's time we started acting like neighbors and care for each other instead of hating each other."

Paul bellowed from inside the truck again. "Don't talk to 'er, Neal. Ya know she's full hatin' on us. I'm warnin' ya, bub."

"I did feel something wrong for you—I'm not sure it was really hate—but I really don't anymore." Her words were true. "I don't think that's the way we're supposed to act. Do you?"

Neal responded quickly. "Why ya doin' this turn around fer now? Why ya' wanna care now? All a sudden." His suspicion laced voice questioned her. "If it's cuz you want us to fix your planes up, well, we don't have no money to fix nuthin'." His eyes narrowed. "Why you doin' this, actin' all nice?"

"Because. That's what my dad would do. And he'd do that because that's what Jesus would do. And those are the footsteps I think, from now on, I'll follow."

Paul stuck his head through the open window and called to his brother. "Are you gonna listen to this hog manure, Neal? Come on, grab the kid and let's git outta here."

Neal hesitated, keeping his eyes fixed on Hailey. He seemed to be rolling her words around in his mind, half confused, half suspicious. After a while, a sorrowful look came over his face and he cocked his head in her direction.

"No. It's time to stop all this hatin' Paul. It's caused nothin' but trouble. An' I'm sick 'n tired of it all."

"Don't talk thata way!" Paul demanded.

Hailey felt for a moment that he might jump right through the window and grab hold of his brother. "You know it's her pa's fault that our pa got kilt. If her pa hadn't asked him to get that tractor unstuck out 'o the mud, Pa wouldn't 'ave fall dead of a heart attack."

Hailey lowered her eyes. She knew that wasn't right. And she was certain Neal knew it, too.

"Paul, that's not 'xactly how it was. It was jus' his time, that's all."

Neal turned to face Hailey. "We'll fix the plane for ya while you're gone, Hailey. And we'll not touch a drink, neither. You got my promise on it."

"I believe you." She held a hand out to him. "And as long as the two of you are in church with your mom and Dee, starting this Sunday, I won't report the vandalism to Sheriff Maxey."

Neal hesitated but finally nodded. "You got my word on that, too. We'll be thar."

Paul threw open the pickup door and then closed it again in a huff. He sank down into the seat with an angry snarl and flapped his arms across his chest.

A few moments later, Hailey was on her way to Cryder, feeling a peace settle over her that she hadn't felt in a long, long time.

It was going to be a long, long drive to Cryder, she knew. But somehow, flying there didn't seem the right thing to do.

CHAPTER SEVENTEEN

Hailey brushed her bangs away from her face as she headed down the long hall to the office marked "Jack Stinson, Vice President."

She halted two steps short of the door, listening to the blustering sound of a male voice coming from the direction she was headed.

"Jack, get these reports out before five and wait for a call from Eddie Lyles, then enter these figures and get us something final on the deal. You may have to try to catch him at home. Then call Steve and Carter and tell them we want a meeting by tomorrow to discuss that new airfoil design. I want something I can look at, not hear about and try to put a picture to on my own. Tell them we have another design firm on the job if you have to. And if Crites calls back—"

A familiar voice intervened. "Hold it, Dad. This is exactly what I've been telling you. There's no way we can continue to run the business this way."

Hailey let out a low whistle and leaned her shoulder blades against the stark white wall. No wonder poor Jack had escaped. She would go raging mad if she had to face this barrage every day. She turned her eavesdropping back to the two men inside the office and held her breath for the explosion she knew must be about to follow.

Instead, she heard a blustering sigh followed by a deep chuckle. "Jack, you know how difficult this is going to be for me. But I'll meet you half way."

Could that be the dad she'd heard about? Marshall Stinson?

The older man cleared his throat. "I'm an old man. Hard to change. This is how I am. But, well, I told you I'd try, and I'm going to try."

"Well, you've always been on the grumpy side."

She heard a muffled, rhythmic thump, no doubt as Jack gave his dad a brisk pat on the back.

"This is a good time for a fresh start for all of us. While Eric's here for the summer, we'll split this load between us, so don't worry about it. Oh, and Dad, don't forget. We knock off at five o'clock."

"Good enough, I suppose. Just let me take a few of these files to my office and I'll get started weeding some paperwork myself." There was a long pause. "I'm working on this, son."

"I know, Dad. Let me know how I can help. We're in this together."

There seemed to be a brief awkward silence. "Ugh, Jack, well, good to have you back. Son. Your mom and I missed you."

Hailey stood motionless, wondering whether to start walking or stay where she was until Marshall Stinson was out of sight. Jack's dad's voice was certainly gruff. Even his admission he missed Jack had been crusty.

But she was pretty sure she detected a hint of…was it humility in Mr. Stinson's voice? She knew what it must have taken for Jack to confront his father with love and honesty, man to man. It was another reason she'd grown to respect Jack. First came friendship, respect, and then…well, then she'd opened her eyes.

• • •

Jack watched his father stride to one of the massive file cabinets and sift through the sea of manila folders. The relief he felt that his father was even willing to attempt to work things out was almost overwhelming.

It was more than overwhelming. It was a miracle. Jack felt a wave of thankfulness. Maybe God listened after all. Hours of prayer and questions had accompanied him on the drive from Barnes to Cryder.

He had learned so much from Hailey. About loyalty. About family. About God.

Her desire to follow her father's dream, even after his death, still touched him. She may have been a bit confused about God's design for her life, but her passion and determination were incredible. Whatever she put her heart into was going to succeed, he had no doubt in his mind.

Jack didn't want to wait until it was too late to work things out with his own dad. He wanted to communicate. To make things better for himself, his brother, and his parents.

He would be here as long as it took, to be a part of returning the business to the honorable, reasonably paced family business it was intended to be. He wanted his father to understand that. Jack might leave again when the time was right to find his own mission. Or maybe the joy of being at Brown Aeronautics would be restored and he'd never want to leave. But one thing he knew for sure: if there was another departure, it would be different from his first. He wouldn't be escaping. He'd be growing. And if he had his way, there was someone special he hoped would be by his side.

Jack took a steady breath of the air around him. He no longer felt smothered by these four walls surrounding him. A keen sense of well-being filled him, and he thanked God for opening his eyes before it was too late.

Marshall Stinson turned to leave, a stack of folders bulging from under one arm. He stopped abruptly at the door and turned to Jack, fishing something from his shirt pocket. He tossed it to Jack. "Almost forgot."

Jack caught it in his right hand and smiled back at his dad as the older man disappeared around the corner with brisk steps.

As Jack absently fiddled with the object, he lifted his head and spied Hailey leaning in the doorframe. His mouth opened in amazement, a mixture of shock and pleasure on his face. "How in the world did you…What are you doing here? Did you just fly in?"

His stunned expression prompted a mischievous smile to ruffle her lips. "I didn't fly. I drove."

She took another step into the office. "It's a really, really long drive."

"Believe me, I know." He stood motionless, staring at her.

She stared back.

"Could we talk for a few minutes?" She motioned to a thick mahogany chair by his desk. "I know how busy you are. But, do you mind?"

"Are you kidding?" A stunned smile finally creased his face and he held the chair for her. "There are some big changes around here. Thanks to you."

She took the seat he offered and set her purse down at her feet. "Thanks to God," she reminded him. "For both of us."

He didn't move. He stood in front of his desk, less than two feet from the woman who had changed his life. *I can't believe this.*

All he wanted to do was hold her. "I'm sorry for leaving you like that. But like I said in the note, we both had things to work out on our own."

"Yes, we did." Her eyes never left his.

"I had to face my father." His voice was certain. "And you had to face yours."

She nodded. "You're right. Again."

"The first thing I did when I returned home was look something up in my Bible." He shook his head. "No, the first thing I did was *find* my Bible. Sure enough it was right where I left it. Buried in the back of my sock drawer. Anyway, I remembered a little plaque my great grandfather always had above his work bench. It was Ephesians 5:1."

"Go on."

He stretched across his desk and gripped a black leather bound Bible. He held it up for her to see. "This Book goes where I go from now on. My manual." He turned the pages quickly. "Ephesians 5:1. Here it is." He relaxed measurably.

"'Follow God's example in everything you do just as a much loved child imitates his father.'"

He closed the book gently, focusing his eyes on her face. "In all my deep thinking lately, I've come to realize that God gave us parents to guide and nurture us into adulthood. But then children must separate themselves from their parents and live as God calls them to live. Those parents aren't perfect. Just humans. They don't always know…"

His voice trailed as he set the Bible on the desk and reached for Hailey, pulling her to her feet. "I don't know why you're here, but I've wanted to see you so badly that my heart aches. I know that my place is here for now, not to follow in my father's professional footsteps, but to be the example of love and patience that my father never had in his life. That's what God wants me to do right now."

"I see."

"No, I don't think you do. I know you're convinced that your place is to follow in your own father's footsteps, but I hope and pray that in the future, if God chooses, that we can be together."

"Jack—"

He pulled her closer. "Don't say it. I want you to know that I'm not going to rush you. I'll wait for you as long as it takes. My prayer is that you'll wait for me."

She tilted her chin up and met his gaze head-on, making no attempt to move away from him. "No, Jack. I won't. I won't wait for you."

"I understand." He let out a slow sigh.

"Jack, I have more than just my father's footsteps to follow. I have my mom's. But most of all, I have Jesus's. And now I truly know exactly where He's leading me."

"Wherever he leads you, Hailey, I hope you'll always be happy." His voice was reconciled. "I hope that your dreams will always come true."

She wrapped her arms around his neck. "I am happy."

"I…I'm glad." He merely stared, tongue-tied at her unanticipated display of affection. "So does that mean everything's going to work out with your business?"

She shrugged with deceptive calm and let her arms drop from his neck. "In a matter of speaking, it has. I've decided to ground the business for now."

"Are you saying that you've given up flying? I'm a little confused. Have you given up the dream?"

"Oh, Jack, the dream wasn't mine to give up. And as for flying, I'd still love to do that. If it's alright with you."

After a few seconds, a dawning smiled etched his face and he dangled the key chain that he still held in his hand.

It was her turn to be astonished.

He gripped her hands in both of his, placing the key chain between her palms. "Here are the keys to your brand new Brown Skycat IV. Along with something else I want you to have."

She opened her hands to find an exquisite diamond ring looped around the gold key chain. Her hands were braced on the edge of the desk in what he assumed was to keep her knees from buckling beneath her. She raised her eyes to meet his brown ones.

Jack scooped her into his arms. "Hailey Holman, will you be my pilot?"

She shook her head slowly. "No, Jack. But I will be your copilot."

About the Author

Beverly Rogers is a southern girl with a heart as big as Texas for God and her family and friends. She's been an award-winning writer since third grade, when she captured first place and a very shiny silver dollar for a poem she wrote in a writing competition. Bev and her husband Bret have three remarkable grown children and the two most wonderful grandchildren in the world, with another on the way. When not writing, Beverly loves spending precious time with her family and whatever will take her outdoors. Visit Beverly at *www.beverlyarogers.com*.

A Sneak Peek from Crimson Romance
(From *Destination Wedding* by Robyn Neeley)

"I do. I do." Wedding planner Kate Ashby quietly repeated her calming mantra. Paralyzed in her window seat, she stared at the illuminated fasten seatbelt sign while her hands gripped the metal buckle strap.

Please turn off. Please turn off. They had to be close to cruising altitude. Soon, she'd be able to request a strong drink to knock her out for the duration of this bumpy flight.

She sat still, trying to ignore the terror pulsating through her. Why hadn't she bought sleeping pills before boarding a twelve-hour flight from New York City to Hawaii? Now, that would have been the smart thing to do.

Glancing out the tiny passenger window, she clutched her gold "K" necklace. It was completely irrational to be terrified and she realized the odds of her and her fellow passengers landing safely in Honolulu were more than in her favor. Still, this was her first time flying such a long duration. Departing Manhattan this evening in turbulent thunderstorms had shot her nerves. She was grateful that her boss had sprung for a first class ticket for the long flight.

A loud rattle caused her to grab hold to her armrests. "What was that?" She turned to the stranger sitting next to her. He had short blondish brown hair and was wearing a blue blazer. His face had a nice tan. She had failed to realize that her row mate was incredibly handsome. Usually the person sitting next to her was a grandparent or couldn't speak English. Perhaps he could help her ease her nerves?

"Um…I think it's the drink cart. Would you like something?" He folded his *Wall Street Journal.*

Sexy and smart.

"I'll take a tequila and tonic," he said to the flight attendant. *And likes his drinks strong. This could be fun.*

She ran her hand along the fabric of her hem, praising herself silently for choosing to wear her white sheath dress and matching jacket. It oozed confidence with each expensive thread. At this point in her career, she had no business wearing such a costly outfit. Although she'd be making partner soon and needed to start dressing the part, at least that's how she rationalized the purchase. It certainly was the perfect outfit for a chance encounter with a handsome businessman.

"Miss, what would you like?" the flight attendant asked.

"Tomato juice, please." She glanced out the window. "How long until we land?"

The flight attendant cracked a smile. "Just eleven and a half short hours."

Kate sighed. "Then can you throw some vodka in?"

The flight attendant handed her a small can of tomato juice and a plastic cup filled with ice cubes. Two tiny vodka bottles were lodged inside. "Here you go. I slipped in an extra one for later. Press that button up there if you need more."

"Thank you." Kate unscrewed one of the bottles and poured it into her cup, swirling it around with her hand. Out of the corner of her eye, she saw the stranger tuck his newspaper into the seat pocket in front of him. Her eyes darted to his ring finger. No wedding band.

He turned to her, and she noticed his sexy full lips and blue eyes. One word to describe him. Hot. Way cuter than any guy she'd ever dated.

"Don't fly much?" he asked and smiled. She caught the small dimple in his right cheek.

"All the—" Her head jolted. Geez. How many turbulent air pockets would they speed through? She grimaced and grabbed the edge of her seat. *Push through it Kate.* "I fly for work all the time but usually only quick trips up and down the west coast."

"Flying never bothers me." He swiveled his glass. "Thanks to my tequila friend, I'll be out like a light in no time."

Mr. Sexy was planning on going to sleep? She should have known. Typical man.

She downed the vodka straight and cracked open the tomato juice, pouring its contents into the empty plastic cup. Unscrewing the second vodka bottle, she added the clear liquid and gave it a swirl. Maybe she could keep him up for a few more minutes until the alcohol fully took effect.

"I'm Kate, by the way."

"Drew." He sipped his drink.

"Nice to meet you." Kate brought the cup to her lips. Why was his name so familiar? She hadn't dated a Drew. Truth be told, she hadn't dated anyone lately. After a number of failed attempts with men who were either only after one thing or just plain wrong for her, she decided to throw herself into her work. It was easier that way.

The plane shook hard, causing her to spill her drink. The tomato juice seeped through her dress, dampening her skin. "Damn it!"

"Here." He handed her his cocktail napkin.

"Thank you." Of course this would happen. She was prone to accidents. Last month, she had spilled an entire glass of wine on a bride's wedding gown right before she walked down the aisle. She blotted her dress. Two hundred dollars—for more confidence—down the drain. Frustration now competed with fear to take over her body.

She bit down on an ice cube while watching the first class flight attendant secure the beverage cart and take her seat. It was never a good sign when they suspended drink service. This couldn't be good. She knew it.

She couldn't help but think about her babies who were waiting for her back home. What if she orphaned them? Who would be their caretaker? Certainly not her mother. Her hands tightened around her seatbelt. "Oh, God. Who's going to raise Carly and Sydney? This is not happening. Please, God. Please. I promise if we land safely I will never ever miss church again. I'll visit my parents every Christmas and stop wasting time tweeting at work."

"Are Carly and Sydney your daughters?"

Kate looked over. She had forgotten about Drew for a second. Was he smirking? Well that's just terrific. He's finding her meltdown humorous. Jerk. He'll wipe that stupid grin off his face when this gigantic metal tube dives nose first into the ground.

"No. They're my cats," she wailed. "My fur babies, and they'll be orphans." She buried her head in her hands.

She felt something hit her leg and moved her hands. It was Drew's seat belt buckle.

"I'll be right back. I need to use the bathroom." He headed for the back of the plane.

"You're not supposed to get up until they turn off the sign," Kate called out. Why couldn't he use the front lavatory? He probably thought she was crazy. She sighed. Maybe she was. Taking a deep breath, she stared up at the illuminated seat belt sign. Figures the one flight she's seated next to a gorgeous man, she's too terrified to flirt.

. . .

Luke Cannon reclined his seat and closed his weary eyes. It had been one whirlwind of a work week. No doubt about it. His reward? Several interrupted hours of much needed sleep. Then again, with was all this swaying he wondered how much shuteye he would actually get.

He often flew for his job working in the family business as his father's right-hand man, but his identical twin brother arranged this trip half-assed at the last possible minute.

Speaking of his mirror image.

"Dude, put this on." Drew approached, peeling off his blazer and throwing it into Luke's lap. He held on to the headrest for balance.

"Why?" Luke raised his eyebrow. What was his brother up to now? He was still pissed at Drew for sticking him in coach while he sat his imperial butt up in first class.

"Look, I need you to switch places with me. You can have my seat up there for the rest of the flight. Plenty of legroom and all the complimentary drinks you want."

Luke cocked his head and peered down the aisle toward the front of the cabin. "You want me to trade seats with you? Why?"

"Because I feel bad for sticking my older bro in coach."

"Yeah, right." Luke was only a few minutes older. A fact Drew seemed to always enjoy pointing out, especially when he wanted something. "Which flight attendant did you piss off already?"

"No one. Come on. Go up there and sit in 3C. The woman next to me is driving me freakin' crazy. She's afraid of flying."

"So wait. You want *me* to sit with the lunatic? Why do I need to pretend I'm you?"

"The flight attendants won't let us switch. I already asked."

"I don't blame them. They're just messing with you. Go sit down."

"I don't think so." Drew thrust his ticket into Luke's hand. "Here, take this and leave yours."

Luke reached for the emergency instructions card in his front seat pocket and pretended to read it. "I don't know. If you want me to spend this whole flight trapped next to a crazy woman…" he glanced at his brother and smirked, "well, I need something in return."

"Really, dude? You're going to do this to me now?" Drew's agitation came through loud and clear.

"And you didn't think that maybe you should have bought me the same first class ticket as yours?"

"Hey, I told you they were sold out. Besides, you're always talking about not spending money." He motioned for Luke to get up. "I'm giving it to you. Take it. All the extra legroom you need."

"Give me your hotel suite and we've got a deal."

"No way. I have big plans for tomorrow night."

"You do?" Luke folded the pamphlet and tucked it in the seat pocket. "Too bad you'll be too exhausted since it looks like you won't be getting any sleep. How many hours left? Ten? Eleven?"

Drew threw his hands up in the air. "Fine. The suite is yours. Lauren's going to be pissed." He motioned for Luke to get up. "Here, go up there now before someone sees us."

"Okay, okay. I'm going. Sheesh." Luke unbuckled his seatbelt and put on the blazer. The flight attendants would probably admonish both of them soon since the captain hadn't turned off the fasten seatbelt sign. "What's her name?"

"Who?"

"The woman you're sitting next to, Casanova."

"Crazy lady? I don't know." He shrugged. "Who cares?"

"You were always the sensitive one." Luke gave his brother a sideways glance.

Drew sat down and buckled his seatbelt. "Thanks, bro, for taking one for the team." He leaned his head back and shut his eyes.

"Yeah, yeah, whatever." Luke started to leave but Drew grabbed his arm.

"Oh, don't ask her about her cats. Whatever you do, do not ask her about her freakin' fur babies."

Luke shook his head and made his way to first class. Since they were kids, Drew and he had played many swap-identity tricks on their parents, teachers, and girlfriends. Being identical had its advantages, particularly for his brother. In high school, they switched senior prom dates after Drew decided his odds of scoring with Luke's date were greater than his own. Drew lost his virginity that night to Luke's chagrin.

"Sir, please sit down." A long-legged flight attendant ordered.

Luke flashed an apologetic smile and counted the rows to 3C. Perhaps, this unexpected seat swapping wouldn't be so bad after all. The flight attendant was certainly pretty.

His hands gripped the back of the seats to steady his balance. He couldn't blame the poor cat lady for being scared with all the rocking.

He crouched down, fully expecting to see a frightened middle-aged spinster dressed in black with grey cat hair all over her.

Wait a second? He glanced up to check that he had the right row. It was the right one, but sitting in 3A was a stunning woman who he guessed could be in her early thirties. The first thing he noticed was her long, wavy brown hair. He'd always had a thing for women with long, dark hair.

This was the vocal terrorist Drew couldn't stand to sit with a minute longer? She wasn't wearing black but a white dress and from what he could tell, her bronze legs might rival those of the flight attendant. Her hands were crunching a tomato juice can while she stared at the fasten seat belt sign. Two empty vodka bottles lay sideways on her folding tray table.

"Hi," he said shyly, sitting down and buckling his seatbelt.

She whipped her head toward him, and her emerald green eyes immediately locked with his. "What took you so long?"

"The tail section broke off," he joked. Judging by her reaction, he knew it was a bad one. "Kidding." He touched her arm.

"I knew that." She glanced at her watch and took a deep breath. "Ten hours and fifty-three minutes to go."

"We're practically ready to prepare for arrival." He chuckled. "So, I'm Drew by the way." The woman shot him a confused look. His brother must have already introduced himself. Figures Drew had told her his name but couldn't remember hers. "I mean you know that already. How do you spell your name again? It's so unusual."

"K-a-t-e."

Kate. Okay, not uncommon. He was going to murder his brother. Confessing that he was Drew's twin was probably the right thing to do but she looked so terrified. He wouldn't know how to explain that his idiot brother had begged him to trade seats. No, he'd continue the charade. It's not like they were going to become friends or start dating. Harmless conversation with a stranger he'd most likely never see again was all this was.

He motioned for the flight attendant. "Would you care for another drink, Kate?" He reached for the crushed tomato juice can still in her hand. "Here, let me take that for you." He noticed that her dress had a large red stain. "Accident?"

"Yep. An expensive one," she said dryly. It was clear she didn't want to talk about it.

"How about joining me in a glass of champagne?"

She shrugged. He took that as a yes.

A few minutes later, the flight attendant brought over two flutes. Luke handed one glass to Kate and raised his. "To bumpy flights with safe landings." He chimed his glass rim to hers.

She took a sip and frowned.

"You don't like it? I can get you something else. What would you like? Some coffee, perhaps?"

"No, it's not that, I…um," she stammered. "I'm sorry."

"For what?"

"You obviously drew the short stick by having to sit next to me." She picked up one of the empty vodka bottles and turned it upside down. "I thought the first drink, or second, would loosen me up. Oh, well. Maybe this will do the trick." She tilted the flute all the way back and finished it. "I hate flying."

"So let's get your mind off of it." Luke moved his armrest up and then reached over. His arm brushed against the top of her dress as he shut the tiny window screen. What he wouldn't give to run his hand underneath it.

Stop it, Luke. The poor woman's having a nervous breakdown.

"How long will you be in Hawaii?" he asked.

"Three weeks. I'm going there for work."

"Wow. I'd like your job." He was happy to hear that this was a business trip and that she wasn't meeting a lover, at least he hoped not. "Do you live in New York, Kate?"

"No, Los Angeles."

Damn. She would live on the west coast. "Were you in New York for business?"

"No. I was visiting my mother to kick some—" Her sentence broke off as the plane hit another air pocket. The airbus dropped down and bounced back up. Luke felt Kate's seatbelt hit him followed by her weight crashing against his leg. She flung her arms around his khakis and hung on for dear life.

"First time flying," he mouthed to the older couple sitting across from them. "Here," he instructed, placing his arm on her back. He unleashed her hands from his leg, guiding her into his arms. "Hold on to me." The scent of her perfume mixed with tomato juice and champagne infiltrated his nostrils. It was surprisingly arousing.

He stroked her hair. "It's going to be fine. You know, pilots like to stay in the air."

"Drew, I don't want to die." She clung to him, burying her head deeper into his chest.

He cringed at the mention of his brother. Should he confess to her that his name was Luke? Now didn't seem like the best time. It would be easier to just continue pretending to be Drew.

He took a deep breath. "Nothing bad is going to happen. I promise you that. If I was worried, I wouldn't—" He paused for a few seconds. How was he going to calm her down and get her back into her seat?

She looked up at him. "Wouldn't what?" Her fearful green eyes pleaded with him to make the rocking stop. His heart fell to his stomach and it wasn't because of the turbulence. He didn't know why, but he had an overwhelming need to protect her.

"Well, I wouldn't do this." He cupped her chin and brought her mouth to his. Her soft lips reacted to his. He deepened the kiss and their tongues moved in sync as the plane continued to sway. When he finally broke the kiss to check on her and catch his breath, he could see she was much more relaxed. "Better?"

She snuggled into his chest and wrapped her arms again around him. "Your heart's beating fast."

"Hmmm." She was right. His heart was racing.

"Drew, I think I had too much to drink. Can you wake me when we land?"

Reclining his seat, he held her as she fell asleep. Who was this beautiful mystery woman in his arms? He smiled. Maybe pretending to be his twin brother would work out in his favor for once.